CW00504457

PURRFECT FOOL

THE MYSTERIES OF MAX 28

NIC SAINT

PURRFECT FOOL

The Mysteries of Max 28

Copyright © 2020 by Nic Saint

All rights reserved. No part of this book may be reproduced in any form by any electronic or mechanical means including photocopying, recording, or information storage and retrieval without permission in writing from the author.

This is a work of fiction. Names, characters, places, brands, media, and incidents are either the product of the author's imagination or are used fictitiously. The author acknowledges the trademarked status and trademark owners of various products referenced in this work of fiction, which have been used without permission. The publication/use of these trademarks is not authorized, associated with, or sponsored by the trademark owners.

Edited by Chereese Graves

www.nicsaint.com

Give feedback on the book at: info@nicsaint.com

facebook.com/nicsaintauthor
@nicsaintauthor

First Edition

Printed in the U.S.A

---

*I*t could have been the perfect nap. The nap to end all naps. Unfortunately there was one thing that detracted from absolute perfection. Or I should probably say one bug: a big, fat fly kept buzzing around my head, making it impossible to enjoy the full benefit of my slumber.

I'd already given this fly the evil eye, but the darn thing didn't seem to be all that quick on the uptake, and just kept at it. Giving it the cold shoulder didn't help either, and so finally I saw no other recourse than to swat at the annoying thing, making my displeasure known not only in word but also in deed.

"Hey, cool your jets, bro!" said the fly, and buzzed off to rob some other pet of sleep.

And so I finally closed my eyes to pick up where I left off when something else intruded upon my much-yearned-for peace and quiet.

Gran came stalking in through the sliding glass door and slammed a newspaper down right next to me, then proceeded to take a seat—unbidden, I might add.

"Will you look at that!" she exclaimed, causing me to

suppress a groan of annoyance and direct a casual glance at said newspaper.

"What is it?" I asked, not in the mood for reading an entire newspaper article and preferring to get the gist straight from the horse's mouth—in this case my human's gran.

"It's that no-good son of mine," the old lady announced, clearly not all that happy with whatever that son of hers had been up to this time. For those of you not in the know, Gran's son is none other than Alec Lip, chief of police in our neck of the woods.

"What did he do?" I asked, more out of politeness and the faint but diminishing hope that this would speed up the process of getting Gran to take her leave and leave me to my hopes and dreams of that catnap I'd been looking so forward to.

"He says he's going to get married! Married, if you please!"

I yawned. "Isn't that a good thing?"

"Not in the same year my granddaughter is tying the knot it isn't!" said Gran. She poked a finger at the newspaper, causing it to crumple. "He's stealing Odelia's thunder, that's what he's doing! How dare he!"

"So maybe you can organize a double wedding? Would save you time and money."

"A double wedding!" Gran cried, clearly aghast at the prospect. "Never in my life will I attend this wedding. Never, you hear me!"

"I hear you," I said, wincing a little, for Gran was even more voluble than usual.

Dooley, who'd been attracted by all the hullabaloo, came prancing over from the pantry, where he'd done his business in his litter box. I could tell he'd done number two, for he had that distinct spring in his step and that merry gleam in his eye he gets when successfully managing to exorcise the product of his mastication and digestion process.

"What's going on?" he asked when he saw Gran's unhappy face. "Did someone die?"

"No, but someone soon will," said Gran with a dark frown at the newspaper.

"Oh, no!" said Dooley, his face falling. "I didn't even know you were sick, Gran. Is it cancer? Or old age?"

Gran gave my best friend a withering look that would have made a more discerning cat wince. "I'm not dying. And for your information, I'm not old. It's my son."

"Oh, no! Does Uncle Alec have cancer?"

"Nobody has cancer!" she cried. "He's getting married!"

Dooley gave me a look of confusion. Usually when humans get married it's cause for cheer, the prospect of a party making everyone happy. But Gran seemed to liken the occasion to a funeral, which was a novel way of looking at the sacred institution.

"Oh, I get it," said Dooley. "Uncle Alec is sick and dying and he wants to get married before he dies." He shook his head sadly. "I liked Uncle Alec. I'll be sad when he's gone."

"Please talk some sense into your friend, Max," said Gran. "I don't have the patience."

"Uncle Alec isn't dying, Dooley," I explained. "He's getting married, and Gran isn't happy about it."

"But why?" asked Dooley, an understandable question. But then his face cleared. "Oh, I know! Charlene is pregnant! And Uncle Alec doesn't want her to have the baby out of wedlock. Just like in that Lifetime movie we saw last week, when Derek the company boss had to marry his secretary Francine when she announced she was pregnant, only she wasn't pregnant, and only said she was so he would marry her. And then when he found out she wasn't pregnant after all, he immediately had the wedding annulled."

Gran gave Dooley a pointed look. "You know, Dooley, that's something that hadn't occurred to me. But you're right. It's the only possible explanation. Charlene must be expecting a baby. Why else would they suddenly announce their wedding plans?"

"Or it could be that Charlene is dying of cancer," Dooley suggested. "And Uncle Alec wants her to die as his wife."

The prospect of her son's betrothed dying a slow and painful death seemed to please Gran, but then she shook her head. "Nah. He would have told me if she was sick." She shrugged. "Which means I'm going to be a grandma soon."

"But... aren't you a grandma already, Gran?" asked Dooley.

"I hope it's a boy," said Gran, ignoring Dooley. "Or twins. A boy and a girl, maybe."

Dooley gave me a look of supreme worry. For some reason he has this idea that if a newborn enters our family, they'll get rid of all the cats. And no matter how many times I've assured him this is simply not the case, he keeps coming back to the horrifying notion.

"Anyway," said Gran, getting up and grabbing her newspaper. "Just thought I'd let you know. I can't tell the rest of the family how I feel about this wedding nonsense, so I hope you'll keep your mouths shut. Not a word to Alec, you hear? Or the others, for that matter."

"My lips are sealed, Gran," I said.

"Your lips look fine to me, Max," said Dooley, studying my lips intently.

"It's just an expression, Dooley," I said. "It means I won't tell anyone what Gran just told us."

"That goes for you, too, Dooley," said Gran. "If word gets out that the groom's mom opposes the wedding, there will be hell to pay."

And with these words, she stomped off again, her face a thundercloud.

Somehow I had the feeling it wouldn't be long before the entire town of Hampton Cove would know exactly how Gran felt about the wedding. We might be able to keep our mouths shut, but would Gran?

"So... let me get this straight," said Dooley. "Uncle Alec is getting married to his girlfriend because she's dying? Or because *he's* dying? Or because she's pregnant?"

"I have no idea, Dooley," I said, still holding out a faint hope to have that nap.

"Or maybe Charlene is dying *and* she's pregnant!" His furry face fell. "I hope she'll be able to deliver the baby before she dies, Max."

"I'm sure that Uncle Alec and Charlene are simply getting married because they love each other," I said. "And that there is no pregnancy and that no one is dying."

"Or it could be that Uncle Alec is pregnant," said Dooley, my reassurances landing on deaf ears as usual. "He looks like he's pregnant, with that very big belly of his."

"Uncle Alec is pregnant?!" suddenly a cry sounded from the kitchen. I looked up and saw that Harriet and Brutus had arrived, the other two cats that make up our household.

Brutus is a butch black cat, and also Harriet's boyfriend,

who's a white Persian. They both looked flabbergasted by this piece of news.

"Uncle Alec can't be pregnant," I said with a laugh. "Men don't get pregnant, you guys."

"I wouldn't be too sure about that, Max," said Brutus. "Nowadays everybody can get pregnant."

"He's right," said Dooley. "I saw a documentary on the Discovery Channel the other night about a man who delivered a healthy baby boy."

"So let me get this straight," said Harriet. "Uncle Alec is pregnant… with a boy?"

I heaved a deep sigh. I had a feeling I wasn't going to get any naptime anytime soon with this lot launching into a discussion on my human's uncle being pregnant.

"As I understand it now," said Dooley, "Uncle Alec is pregnant, and his future wife Charlene is also pregnant, *and* dying, which is why they're tying the knot in a hurry."

Harriet's eye went a little wider. "Uncle Alec and Charlene are getting married?"

"Yeah, looks like it," I said. At least that part of the story was undoubtedly true.

"But… he can't get married!" said Harriet. "Odelia and Chase are getting married. Uncle Alec can't steal her thunder —it's just not fair!"

"Exactly what Gran said," I agreed, nodding. I watched that fat fly flit hither and thither, and was already yearning for the good old days when it had been just me and it.

"We have to do something about this, you guys!" said Harriet, getting all worked up now. "We can't let this wedding take place!"

"It has to take place," said Dooley. "Because Charlene and Uncle Alec are both dying, and they're both pregnant, too, so they have to get married before it's too late."

"Dooley!" said Harriet. "Are you serious?!"

I felt it was time to intervene before things got completely out of hand. "Look, the only thing we know for sure is that a wedding has been announced and will be taking place between Uncle Alec and Charlene," I said. "The rest is just idle speculation."

"But—" said Dooley.

"Idle speculation," I repeated emphatically.

As I'd expected, my words acted like oil on the raging waters of Harriet's indignation and Dooley's rampant imagination, and for a few moments a pleasant silence reigned.

Then Dooley said, "Maybe Odelia is pregnant, too, and very soon she'll kick us all out, because everybody knows that cats and babies don't mix, so there's that to consider."

"Oh, Dooley," I said, and that big fly, which had taken advantage of me being distracted by landing on the tip of my nose, said, "If you want, I can go and find out for you, cat."

And I said, "Wait, what?"

The fly shrugged and said, "Haven't you ever heard the expression 'Fly on the wall' before? Well, I can be that fly for you, cat."

So I said, "Sure. Why not?"

Anything to get rid of this fly. Now if only I could get rid of my housemates, but somehow I had a feeling this wasn't in the cards.

The life of a fly is often a pretty lonely life—and a short one, too. So Norm, as he buzzed off on his mission, was actually happy with this change of scenery. His brethren and sistren might content themselves by eating dirt, but Norm was that rare fly who had, from the moment he was born, entertained higher aspirations. He'd always envisioned himself as that rare breed of fly: the adventurous type. And overhearing those cats speculating about their humans, Norm had smelled an opportunity and grabbed it.

So first he buzzed off in the direction of the house next door, where that old woman had disappeared to, and decided to pick up some little tidbits of raw intelligence there, just like James Bond would, if James Bond was about half an inch in diameter and consisted of an exceedingly hairy body, six hairy legs, two compound eyes and some extra-sensitive antennae. Though in all honesty all that Norm had in common with James Bond was a hairy chest and that can-do attitude your average British spy has in spades.

And he was in luck, as Grandma Muffin had just grabbed

her purse and was on her way out the door, so he simply followed in her wake, hoping it would lead to something.

He landed on top of her head, before being rudely swatted away—the life of a fly consists mainly of being swatted away—and ducked into her car just as she did.

"Stupid fly," Grandma Muffin muttered as she gave Norm one of her trademark dark looks, then started up the engine, and floored the accelerator, causing the car to lurch away from the curb at a much higher rate of speed than traffic cops like to see.

Moments later, it seemed, they were already cruising through downtown Hampton Cove, and when the older lady steered her car into an underground parking garage, Norm was buzzing with anticipatory glee. Looked like he was in for a real treat!

Maybe a meeting with some Deep Throat type informant? A showdown in the bowels of what looked like a boutique hotel? He didn't know what would follow, but had a feeling it was going to be good. So it was with a slight sense of disappointment that he watched Grandma Muffin simply park her car, get out and slam the door then walk off.

They took the elevator up to the hotel lobby, and once again Norm's hopes soared: a secret meeting in one of the hotel rooms with a foreign spy? A dead drop in one of the hotel's garbage bins of some secret documents? So when the old lady Max called 'Gran' met up with a gorgeous redhead with plunging décolletage in the hotel lobby, and the both of them walked into the dining area, he knew this was it. The redhead was probably a Russian spy, here to hand over the secrets to the Russian rocket program, or maybe even spike Grandma's drink with a little-known nerve agent or truth serum!

So when both women took a seat in the outside dining area and ordered drinks from a suspicious-looking waiter—

a Korean spy? A Chinese double agent?—he was on the lookout for the little vial containing the deadly nerve agent, and ready to warn Gran!

"We gotta do something, Scarlett," said Gran. "We have got to stop this wedding."

"But why?" said the woman named Scarlett, tossing her red curls across her shoulders. She was dressed in a provocatively cleavaged red dress and red high heels, her lips a very bright Scarlett and looking every bit the sexy Russian secret agent.

"Why? Are you kidding me? They're going to ruin Odelia's wedding!"

"I think it's pretty cute. And you can always make it a double wedding," said Scarlett, taking a sip from her drink—a flat white, if Norm had followed the proceedings closely. So far no little vials with deadly nerve agents were in evidence but that could happen any moment now.

"Trust me on this, Scarlett. Alec wouldn't be getting married if he wasn't being coerced—if Charlene wasn't putting a knife to his throat." She slapped the table, causing her own drink—hot cocoa with plenty of cream, from the looks of it—to dance up and down. "That woman's got something on my son and I want to know what it is."

"Isn't it possible that they simply love each other and want to celebrate that love by tying the knot?" asked Scarlett, who was clearly a romantically inclined Russian spy.

"Oh, Scarlett, Scarlett," said Gran. "I see she's gotten to you, too."

"Nobody's 'gotten' to me, Vesta. I just think they make a damn fine couple, and I wish them all the future happiness in the world, and frankly I think you should, too."

"He's too old to get married!"

"He's only, what, fifty-something?"

"I'm telling you Alec would never get married if he wasn't

being hoodwinked. And I want to know what that woman is holding over him."

Scarlett shrugged. "Can only be one thing."

Vesta gave her a scathing look. "You've got a one-track mind, Scarlett."

"What? I'm telling you—in my experience there's only one thing that would make a man want to propose marriage to a woman and that's—"

"Don't say it. Don't you dare say it."

"Sex! What else?"

"I'm the man's mother, Scarlett!"

"So? There are certain realities you just have to face, Vesta. Charlene is an attractive woman, and I'm sure she's got assets that would make any man happy to explore them."

Gran buried her face in her hands. "Oh, God."

"It's human nature!"

"Just because you're obsessed with sex doesn't mean we all are."

"Just saying," said Scarlett with a shrug.

Norm was losing his patience. So far nothing was happening that would make James Bond bother to get out of bed in the morning, and he was starting to wonder if Max had sent him on a fool's errand. He wouldn't put it past the cat to try and get rid of him.

"Look, I want to find out what Charlene's got on my son, and then I want to stop that wedding from happening. Are you with me or not, that's all I need to know right now."

"Well…" said Scarlett, wavering.

"It's going to break my granddaughter's heart, Scarlett! And I happen to love my granddaughter—more than anything in the world!"

"Aww," said Scarlett, regarding her friend with interest.

"What's the look for?"

"So you do have a heart."

"Of course I have a heart!" She then wagged a finger in her friend's face. "But don't you go and blab about it. It would ruin my reputation."

"Okay, fine. I'll help you. What do you want me to do?"

"First we need to find out Charlene's secret."

"And how do you propose we do that?"

"Easy. We spy on her."

"What do you mean?"

"We bug her phone, her house, her office, we put a tracker on her car..."

"Isn't that, like, extremely illegal?"

"Who cares? I'm trying to protect my family here, Scarlett!"

"Fine! But aren't you forgetting one thing?"

"What?"

"We're not exactly professional spies, you and me. So how do you propose we pull this off?"

Grandma Muffin smiled. "Leave that to me. I've got it all figured out."

Okay, so it wasn't exactly the high-profile spy bonanza Norm had anticipated, but he still felt, as he started the long flight back to Harrington Street to report to Max, that he'd gleaned some interesting intelligence. And he was starting to see that he'd landed himself in exactly the kind of spy story Mr. Bond would have appreciated.

4

_____

$\mathcal{M}$arge looked at her watch, then up and down the street. Her husband was late. They'd arranged to go shopping together and so far Tex was a no-show. She frowned as she thought about the article she'd just read on the Gazette website. Breaking news, it said. The Chief of Police was getting married to the Mayor, it said. A thousand comments had already been posted, and almost all of them heralded the news and wished the future husband and wife all the happiness in the world.

Marge had tried to call her brother, wanting to ask him what he thought he was doing, letting her find out about his upcoming wedding from the Gazette. But he wasn't picking up, and nor was her daughter Odelia, who'd written the article in the first place.

What was going on here?

Finally Tex came hurrying up, looking apologetic. "I'm sorry!" he said as he joined her on the sidewalk. "Have you been waiting long?"

"Ten minutes," she said. "What took you so long?"

"Ida Baumgartner," he said ruefully, and she smiled. It was

just Tex's luck to get his most faithful patient to pay him a visit just before he needed to be somewhere.

"What did she suffer from this time?" she asked. "Probably some disease that hasn't been invented yet?"

"Actually this time she was suffering from something real," said her husband as they walked into Darling's Dress Code. "A rash. On her face."

"Probably an allergy."

"I don't think so. She did mention she was using a new face cream so—"

But Marge was already making a beeline for the shoe department and forgot all about Ida Baumgartner and her long string of real or imagined illnesses. The store was organizing a big sale today, and she wanted to get two pairs of shoes for Tex, and a pair for her as well. Initially she'd wanted to buy them for their daughter's wedding, but now that it looked like her brother was getting hitched, too, they'd have to do double duty.

"Read this and tell me what you think," she said once her husband's shoe needs had been taken care of and she entered the frantic fray to find a nice pair for herself.

When she returned with a pair of elegant pink pumps—not exactly ideal for a wedding but the price was so right!—he handed her back her phone, looking stumped.

"I don't get it," he announced. "Your brother is getting married?"

"That's what it looks like."

"And you didn't know about this?"

"Nope. He didn't tell me a thing." In fact she'd talked to her brother the night before, and he hadn't given any indication that he was about to tie the knot again—fifteen years after becoming a widower.

Tex looked as flummoxed as she was feeling. "I tried to

call him," she said, "but he's not picking up. And then I tried calling Odelia, but she's not picking up either."

"So... maybe the article is a hoax?"

"Odelia wrote it," she pointed out.

"Oh." Her husband shook his head. "Then I don't get it." He answered in the affirmative when she paraded in front of him with a pair of black strappy heels, though his mind seemed elsewhere, and presumably not with Ida Baumgartner's peculiar rash. "He could have told us," he said. "If he's going to get married at the same time as Odelia we should probably organize a double wedding. Two weddings in a row seems silly."

"Yeah, that's what I was thinking. We'd better make it a double wedding." Though preferably she would have liked her brother to postpone his wedding. He was totally going to steal his niece's thunder now, which seemed like a really selfish thing to do.

Unless there was something she didn't know? Some reason her brother suddenly felt the need to get married?

"Maybe Charlene is pregnant?" Tex suggested, clearly thinking along the same lines as she was.

"Can I help you?" suddenly the salesgirl said, materializing next to her.

"Do you have these in a bigger size?" she asked. She liked the shoes, but they were a little tight.

The girl disappeared, in search of the shoes, and Marge took a seat next to her husband. "How old is Charlene?"

"Your age, right?"

"That's what I thought. Is it even possible to be pregnant at forty-eight?"

"It's possible," said her husband the doctor. "Unlikely but possible. Though I didn't know they were trying for a baby."

"No, me neither. Unless..." They shared a look of consternation.

"Unless it was an accident?"

"Could be," she said. "Though nowadays people don't get married just because they're expecting a baby, do they?"

"Not usually," Tex allowed. "Unless they've decided it's best for the baby if the parents are married before it arrives into this world."

"But if she is pregnant, wouldn't she have told you? You are her doctor, right?"

"Yeah, but I haven't seen her in a while. Ever since she got involved with Alec she's been seeing a doctor in Hampton Keys."

"She probably feels weird about seeing you now that you're practically family." They let the notion of Alec becoming a father hang in the air for a moment, then Marge nudged her husband. "You could find out though, couldn't you? I mean, from one doctor to another, and Charlene technically still being your patient and all?"

"I could find out," said Tex, nodding. "But it wouldn't exactly be ethical for me to—"

"Call him," said Marge. "Call him now."

"But honey!"

"He's my brother, Tex. I have a right to know. So either you call him or I'll do it."

Tex sighed, hesitated for a moment, then took out his phone and placed the call. The conversation was short and to the point, and when Tex hung up the phone he said, "Nope. She's definitely not pregnant."

"So then why? Why the sudden haste?"

$\mathcal{O}$ delia arrived home feeling a little dejected. She didn't begrudge her uncle his future happiness with his new bride, but she just wished he'd told her the news in person instead of having the Mayor send an email to her boss, who had then forwarded her the email and asked her to write a short article announcing the happy occasion.

She took a bottle of cold water from the fridge and poured herself a glass of the cooling liquid. And as she leaned against the kitchen counter, she saw that four cats were all staring at her expectantly. She smiled.

"Let me guess. Your bowls are empty?"

But when she glanced over she saw that her darlings still had plenty of kibble.

"So tell us already, Odelia!" said Harriet, who had the least patience of all of her cats. "Is it really true that Uncle Alec is getting married? And if so why?"

"And is he pregnant or is Charlene pregnant or are they both pregnant?" asked Brutus.

"Or are they both pregnant *and* dying?" asked Dooley.

In spite of herself, she laughed. It was just like her cats to come up with these crazy stories. "Frankly I have no idea," she said.

"But you wrote the story!" said Harriet. "Gran said so herself!"

"Yeah, I wrote the story, but only because my editor asked me to. He received an email from the Mayor's Office, announcing the wedding, and that's all I know."

"The Mayor's Office?" asked Max with a frown. "You mean Uncle Alec didn't personally tell you the news?"

She swallowed. "No, he didn't. And when I tried to call him he didn't pick up. So at this point I know just as much as you guys. Which is exactly nothing."

"But... he's your uncle," Dooley pointed out.

"Thanks, Dooley," she said. "I didn't know that."

Dooley stared at her. "You didn't know?"

"Of course I know, silly!"

"So... he *has* to talk to you, right?"

She shrugged. The whole thing had surprised her, but she wasn't the kind of person to fret, so she just told herself there was probably a perfectly good reason why her uncle hadn't told her the news in person, and why he was refusing to take her calls.

And just as she took another sip of water, the doorbell chimed and she placed down the glass and went to answer the door. She was surprised to find Charlene Butterwick on the mat, looking distraught. Her hair was a mess, and she had dark rings under her eyes. "Can I come in?" the Mayor asked, and walked in without waiting for Odelia's reply.

"What's going on?" asked Odelia when Charlene quickly glanced over her shoulder before closing the door.

"It's your uncle," said Charlene, then suddenly burst into tears. "He-he's been taken, Odelia."

"What?!" Odelia cried. "What do you mean?"

"He's been kidnapped. By some very bad people. And now I don't know what to do."

"Sit down," said Odelia as she led the highly distraught mayor to the couch in the family room and sat her down. "Now tell me exactly what happened."

Charlene nodded, and gratefully accepted the glass of water and took a sip. "It happened last night. We were at my place watching TV when suddenly the doorbell rang. Since it was almost midnight I was reluctant to open the door, so Alec went to go look instead. And before I knew what was happening, suddenly three men forced their way inside. They were holding a gun on Alec and then on me, too, and told us to sit down. They proceeded to gag us and tie us up and then started ransacking the house, looking for who knows what. Money, probably, though I could have told them they were in for a disappointment, since I'm not exactly a rich woman. Next thing I knew they grabbed Alec and forced him up from the couch…" She gave Odelia a teary look. "And that's the last time I saw him. They led him out of the house, I heard a door slam, and a car drive off."

"My God," said Odelia, clutching a hand to her face. "And this was last night?"

Charlene nodded. "Before they left they made me swear not to call the police. They said if I did, I'd never see Alec again. And I believe them." She shook her head. "And then they said the weirdest thing. They told me to contact the press, and announce my upcoming wedding to your uncle. They even gave me a document with detailed instructions I had to follow to the letter. So I did. I sent out the email immediately after they left. I was afraid if I didn't, they'd…" She swallowed with difficulty. "They'd kill him."

"Charlene, but that's terrible!"

"I know. I went to work today, also as instructed, but I

couldn't help think about what happened. I was a total mess. Still am."

"And they haven't contacted you since last night?"

The Mayor shook her head. "I haven't heard from them or your uncle. And now I fear the worst."

The front door opened and closed and Chase walked in. When he caught sight of Charlene and the state she was in, he immediately came over. "What's wrong?" he asked. "Is this about the wedding?"

Charlene glanced at Odelia, then up at Chase, and Odelia understood her meaning. "You can trust Chase, Charlene," she said. "He won't tell anyone."

Charlene nodded, then said, in a choked voice, "Alec's been kidnapped, Chase. They took him last night and..." She broke into tears. "I think he just might be dead!"

6

"*W*hat's going on, Max?" asked Dooley. "I don't understand."

"Charlene just told Odelia that Uncle Alec has been kidnapped," I said.

"I know, but that can't be right, right?"

"Why not?" I said. "Everyone can be kidnapped."

"Yes," said Brutus. "Uncle Alec has just as much right to be kidnapped as anyone else."

"But… Uncle Alec is the chief of police," said Dooley. "And police chiefs don't just get kidnapped. There are rules against that sort of thing."

"I'm sure there are rules against anyone being kidnapped," I pointed out, "but that doesn't prevent kidnappers from still taking people."

"But… why?"

It was the exact same question Chase now asked the stricken mayor of our town, even as Odelia handed her a box of Kleenex.

"I don't know," said Charlene. "All I know is that they said I wasn't to call the police and tell them what happened." She glanced up at Chase. "Please don't tell anyone? I don't want anything to happen to Alec." She closed her eyes. "If it's not too late already."

"Can you give me a description of the kidnappers?" asked Chase, taking a seat next to the Mayor and taking out his notebook. "Or the make and model of their car?"

Charlene shook her head. "All three of them were pretty big guys, but since they were wearing masks I can't really tell you what they looked like."

"Clothes? Shoes? Anything that stands out?"

Charlene thought for a moment, then said, "The one who seemed to be in charge was wearing red Converse shoes. I remember looking down at them and thinking they looked really nice. They looked new, too."

Chase wrote this down in his little notebook, but I didn't see how this would help him in any way. I'll bet many people wear those kinds of shoes.

"Anything else?" he prompted gently.

"I–I think he spoke with an accent. I couldn't really place it at the time, but now I think it might have sounded as if he was from… Boston?"

"Boston," Chase repeated, and jotted this down, too.

"I don't get it," said Odelia. "Why would anyone kidnap my uncle? He's not rich, he doesn't own any property, and as far as I can tell he doesn't have any enemies."

"Are you sure about that?" asked Chase. "As a policeman he must have made some enemies over the course of his career."

"Well, sure," said Odelia. "But so have you. So has any cop on the force. So why him?"

Just then, the big fly who'd been annoying me to no end came buzzing in through the open window, and settled down on the couch seat next to me. "Max, I have some excellent pieces of intelligence for you," the fly announced.

"That's great," I said, and if I was a little distracted it was because I was more interested in what Odelia and Chase were discussing with the Mayor than anything this fat fly had to offer.

"Don't you want to know what I discovered?" asked the fly, sounding disappointed.

"Yeah, the thing is—my human's uncle has just been kidnapped," I explained. "So we're a little busy right now, Mr. … what's your name exactly?"

"Norm," said the fly.

"Great. Now if maybe you could come back a little later, that would be—"

"They're going to try and stop the wedding!" Norm blurted out.

"What wedding? What are you talking about?" I said, and it was a testament to my distress that I'd completely forgotten about the upcoming wedding, spectacularly revealed in that morning's Gazette.

"Your Uncle Alec and the Mayor," said Norm. "Grandma Muffin and her friend Scarlett are going to stop the wedding any way they can. But first they're going to spy on Charlene—bug her house, her office, her car… Looks like they'll bug the works. And can I just say I object to this word 'bug?' It just seems unnecessarily derogatory and offensive."

I stared at the fly, and so did my friends.

"Who is your new buddy, Max?" asked Brutus.

"Oh, this is Norm," I said. "Norm, meet Harriet, Brutus and Dooley, my friends and housemates."

"Hi, Norm," said Brutus. "I didn't even know flies could talk."

"Oh, we can talk all right," said Norm. "Now if you still want me to carry on with my mission I'm afraid I'm going to have to ask you for some form of remuneration, Max. I can't keep working gratis, you know. I may just be a fly, but I still have my standards."

"Remuneration?" I asked. "What do you mean?"

"Food, Max!" said the large fly. "Nourishment!"

"Oh-kay," I said, a little reluctantly. "So what do you want?"

The fly hovered up and down, then said, "A sample of your stool would be nice."

"Deal," I said quickly. It seemed like a small sacrifice to make to ask Odelia not to clean out our litter box until Norm had done his sampling.

"Did you just say you want our stool, Norm?" asked Dooley.

"Sure. Like it or not, but it's one of my main sources of nourishment, little buddy. Now what do you want me to do, Max? In other words: what's my next assignment?"

"But... stool is dirty!" said Dooley. "Stool is not to be sampled but thrown out!"

"That's where you're wrong, buddy," said the fly. "As the saying goes: one man's stool is another man's gourmet meal."

I was pretty sure the saying didn't exactly go like that, but I was already happy we could avail of Norm's compound eyes and his sharp ears, especially now that we were suddenly faced with a family crisis of epic proportions.

"Look, Uncle Alec has been kidnapped," I told the fly. "So whatever you can find out that will lead us to the kidnappers, that would be wonderful, Norm. Anything at all."

"Gotcha, Max!" said the fly excitedly. "I'm on it!" And promptly he buzzed off again.

I noticed how Harriet was staring at me, her mouth slightly agape. "Did you just conduct an entire conversation... with a dung fly, Max?" she asked.

"I'm not sure he's a dung fly," I said, staring after Norm. "He could just be a housefly."

"Answer the question!"

"Why, yes, I guess I did," I admitted. "Norm is good people, Harriet. And I'm sure he'll find out what we need to know about this kidnapping business. Plus, he's cheap. Who else will investigate a case in exchange for a little bit of poo, if you see what I mean."

"I don't believe this," said Harriet. "Just when you think you've seen it all..."

7

"*My* poor brother!" said Mom. "We have to call in the FBI, the army—the National Guard!"

"We're not calling anyone," said Odelia decidedly. "We don't want to endanger my uncle's life."

"But—"

"It's best if we do as the kidnappers say, honey," said Dad, placing a soothing hand on his wife's arm.

They were all seated around the living room table, a table rarely used, as Odelia and Chase liked to eat their meals at the kitchen counter. Odelia and Chase were there, of course, and so were Odelia's mom and dad, and also Charlene. Gran wasn't present, nor did they want her to be. They'd immediately decided that given the old lady's age and attachment to her son it was best not to tell her what had happened to her dear Alec.

"So what do we do now?" asked Dad, directing his question at Charlene. "Did they give you any more instructions, apart from that wedding announcement?"

"They said they'd be in touch," said Charlene, whose eyes

were red and so was her nose. "I really wish I knew what they're up to. What this is all about."

"All I can think is that this is some kind of revenge," said Mom. "Someone my brother arrested and put behind bars who now wants to take revenge." She directed a questioning look at Chase. "Maybe you can find out if anyone that Alec arrested has been released from prison recently? Someone bearing a grudge?"

"Good idea," said Chase, nodding. "I'll look into it."

"But be discreet about it," Charlene implored. "I don't want these kidnappers to find out I've been talking to you—a cop."

"I'm not here as a cop now, Charlene," said Chase. "I'm here as a family member."

"And Uncle Alec's godson," said Odelia, who hadn't forgotten the reason Chase had come to town in the first place, when his high-flying NYPD career had tanked and he'd needed a place to lick his wounds and start over again.

"Alec gave me a fresh start," said Chase now. "He helped me out when I was at the end of my rope. Gave me a place to stay and a job. I'd do anything for that man. So if you don't mind I'm going to ghost your phone, Charlene."

"Ghost my phone?" asked Charlene.

"It means he'll know when the kidnappers call you, and he'll be able to see what they say when they send you a message," Odelia explained.

"Oh, right," said Charlene, nodding distractedly. "Honestly, I'm supposed to go into work tomorrow, but I don't feel like I can. People will know something is wrong, and they'll ask me all kinds of questions about the wedding and I simply don't know what to tell them."

"They'll simply think you're still bowled over with Alec's wedding proposal," said Mom. "And if you lock yourself up in your office they'll leave you alone. Unless you have a meeting scheduled?"

"No, nothing special," said Charlene. She rubbed her face. "Oh, this is just a nightmare, isn't it?"

It absolutely was, Odelia thought, and glanced over to her cats. She hoped they would be able to help find her uncle. In fact they were probably her only hope, as the family couldn't use police resources, and Chase would have to be very discreet lest he alert the kidnappers.

She looked down at her phone and wondered now if they were being watched—or overheard?

And if they were, how were they to find out?

"Did… did these kidnapers do something with your phone?" she asked Charlene.

But the Mayor shook her head. "I don't think so. Though they did take your uncle's phone when they marched him out."

Which just stood to reason, of course. And which explained why all of Odelia's calls had gone straight to voice-mail. Then she got an idea. "Can you trace my uncle's phone somehow?" she asked Chase.

"I already did," said the cop. "But no dice. Looks like they switched it off and removed the battery. So no way to trace him through his phone, I'm afraid."

These crooks seemed to have thought of everything, which just proved that Mom's theory was probably correct: most likely these were gangsters her uncle had put away at some point in his long career, and who were now out to take revenge on him.

But then why the wedding announcement?

What were they up to?

Just then, Gran came breezing into the room, and when she found all of them seated around the table looking glum, she frowned. "What's going on?" she asked. Then when she saw Charlene's teary face, her frown deepened. "Is the wedding off? Is that it?"

"No, the wedding isn't off," said Charlene, and wiped away a tear.

"So where is he? Where is that son of mine, who didn't even have the decency to tell his sweet old mother in person about his upcoming nuptials?"

"Alec is... at work," said Charlene, casting a quick glance at Odelia. For a politician she wasn't very adept at lying, the latter thought.

"Yeah, he's working late," she said.

"Hrmph," said Gran. "So why the shotgun wedding is what I'd like to know." When they all stared at her, she added, "Well? Is it true what they're saying?"

"What are they saying?" asked Mom.

"That Madam Mayor got a bun in the oven!" said Gran, who never beat about the bush and wasn't beating about the bush now.

Charlene barked a curt laugh. "Me! Pregnant! As if!"

"No baby?" asked Gran, looking slightly disappointed. "Then why? Why the rush? And why this weird-ass announcement?"

Charlene shrugged. "I'm Mayor, Vesta, and Alec is Chief of Police. When two public figures such as ourselves decide to tie the knot the public has a right to be informed."

"Oh, I'm sure they do, but what about me? Don't you think the mother of the groom has a right to be informed?" She gestured to Odelia's mom. "Or the man's own sister?"

"Ma," said Mom warningly.

"No, I'm just curious," said Gran. "My own son is getting married, and he doesn't even tell me in person? I have to read about it in the newspaper, same as everyone else?"

"I'm truly sorry," said Charlene. "It's just that..."

"Alec was going to tell you, but it slipped his mind," said Mom. "Isn't that right, Charlene?"

Charlene nodded. "Yeah, we discussed it last night, and I told him: you better call your mom and tell her. But he must have forgotten."

"Hrmph," said Gran, but looked slightly mollified as she crossed her arms in front of her chest. "Typical Alec. Always forgetting his dear old mother." She directed a pointed look at her daughter. "So when did you find out?"

"Same as you," said Mom. "When I read about it in the paper."

"When I get my hands on that son of mine, he's going to wish he was never born," vowed Gran, and took out her phone. But when she placed it to her ear, she announced, "Damn voicemail again." Then, speaking into her phone: "Pick up, Alec. It's your mother." She listened for a moment, then said, "Oh, so that's how it is, huh? Well, you're dead to me, too! And don't even bother inviting me to your wedding, cause I'm not coming!"

And with these words, she disconnected and stalked out.

8

"There's something they're not telling me, Scarlett," Vesta spoke into her phone as she got into her car. "You should have seen the look on Charlene's face. She'd clearly been crying her eyes out. And my son isn't picking up his phone."

"That's bad," said Scarlett. "So what are you going to do?"

"We're going full steam ahead with our plans, that's what. Did you get the stuff?"

"I did. Though the guy at the store gave me a strange look when I asked for half a dozen of those listening bugs. So I told him I'm going to use them to spy on my boyfriend figuring he's been two-timing me with my best friend. He thought that was hilarious."

"Quick thinking. Good. We don't need any nosy parkers sticking their noses where they don't belong. So I'll meet you there, all right?"

"Are you sure about this, Vesta? Technically we are breaking the law."

"We're the neighborhood watch, honey. We *are* the law."

And as she ended the call and started up the engine she

got another idea. A real doozie. Bugging Charlene's home and office wasn't enough. She needed something more to really lay bare the woman's deceitfulness and treachery. And she knew exactly what.

So she shut down the car again and stalked into the house, only to find the meeting still in full swing. And as she'd suspected, the conversation immediately died down the moment she entered the house. They were all in it together! Her own family—all of them conspiring against her!

"Dooley!" she snapped. "Come!"

"Why?" asked Dooley.

"No questions," she said curtly. "Come with me. Right now."

"But…" He cast a worried look at his friend and Gran rolled her eyes.

"All right—fine! Max, you come, too."

"Where are you taking my cats?" asked Odelia suspiciously.

"None of your business," Vesta barked.

Two could play this game, she thought. If they were going to start keeping secrets from her, she would simply turn the tables on them. See how they liked them apples!

Max and Dooley followed her out into the corridor, then out of the house.

The moment they were safely ensconced in the car, she turned and said, a gleam in her eye, "have I got the mission for you guys!"

<hr>

I don't know about you, but every time Gran gets that strange slightly feverish gleam in her eyes it's time for me to start worrying about her sanity and about my safety.

"What is it, Gran?" asked Dooley, who seemed as worried about this strange behavior of Odelia's grandmother as I was. "Where are you taking us?"

"You know about that wedding announcement that went out this morning, right? My son getting married to Charlene Butterwick?"

"Uh-huh," I said, nodding.

"Well, for some reason or another he and Charlene are being extremely secretive about the whole sordid affair, and I'm on a mission to find out what's going on."

I could have told her what was going on, but I was under strict instructions not to reveal anything to Grandma Muffin, for fear her poor heart wouldn't be able to take the strain. I wasn't so sure her heart was as weak as all that, though. But I wasn't going to go against Odelia's wishes, so I merely nodded obediently. "So what do you suggest?"

"I'm going to bug Charlene's apartment, her office, her phone, her car, in fact I'm going to bug that woman's entire life, and then I'm going to follow her around wherever she goes, and find out once and for all how she's managed to force my son into this shotgun wedding. Cause if I know Alec, and I think I do, it's pretty obvious he would never jump into this thing without being coerced."

"You think Charlene is forcing Uncle Alec to get married?" asked Dooley.

"Of course she is! Isn't it obvious! The conniving little trollop is manipulating my son into a marriage he doesn't want! And it's my job as his mother to get him out of this predicament if it's the last thing I do."

"Okay," I said, a little uncertainly. Rarely had I ever known a human to be so completely wrong about something. "So what do you want us to do?"

"I'm going to insert you into Charlene's life and you're going to feed me information. A bug can't pick up everything, but two feline spies can." She gave us a beaming smile, as if expecting a warm round of applause.

"So… you want us to go live with Charlene?" I asked, still not seeing the full picture.

"Bingo! You're my wedding present to that treacherous woman, but secretly you'll report to me the whole time. And to that end…" And before I knew what was going on, she was suddenly strapping a collar around my neck. A collar, if you please!

"Hey!" I said, shocked and not a little bit surprised. "What are you doing?!"

"Oh, don't be a baby, Max," she growled. "What does it look like I'm doing? I'm giving you a collar. And Scarlett is going to put a bug inside that collar."

"A bug!" said Dooley. "But I don't like bugs. Bugs can kill you!"

"Not that kind of bug," said Gran as she placed a collar around Dooley's neck, too. "There. That should do the trick. Now all we need to do is to make sure the connection is A-Okay and we're ready to get this show on the road."

I didn't know what show she was referring to, or even what road, exactly, but I was already pretty sure I wasn't going to like either show or road. And as she drove off, practically taking out Kurt Mayfield's mailbox as she did, I shared a look of extreme distress with Dooley. Suddenly we'd been thrust in the middle of an adventure we hadn't bargained for.

And the worst part? We were going to be introduced into the home of the woman who'd just been the victim of a home invasion!

Yikes!

9

"*I* wonder what Gran is planning to do with Max and Dooley," said Harriet as she watched Gran take off.

"Probably run some errands," said Brutus.

"I doubt it. You know what I think? I think Gran knows what's going on, and she's just recruited Max and Dooley to help her find her son."

"Sounds plausible."

"Well, it's not fair. Why is she recruiting Max and Dooley and leaving us behind?"

"Because… Dooley is hers?" Brutus suggested.

"Yeah, I know, but Max isn't. So why does he get to go and not us? And have you noticed how Odelia hasn't even told us to help her find her uncle? We're being railroaded here, Brutus. Simply put out to pasture. And I'm not standing for it."

"Standing for what?" asked Brutus, who seemed content just to lie there on the couch and do nothing whatsoever. The whole situation frankly infuriated the prissy Persian.

"Come on," she said now.

"Come where? "asked Brutus, alarmed.

"We're going to find Uncle Alec before Max and Dooley do, and prove once and for all that we're the premier sleuths here, and not them."

But... nobody asked us," said Brutus, causing Harriet to give him a furious look.

"*I'm* asking you, Brutus. In fact I'm *telling* you. Let's go and find Uncle Alec before he's delivered back to his family in lots of little pieces."

"Little pieces!" Brutus cried, horrified by the word picture she was painting.

"Didn't you hear what Odelia said? Uncle Alec has been kidnapped by professional criminals. The kind that like to outfit their victims with shoes made of concrete and dump them in the nearest river. Or dissolve their bodies in a bath filled with acid. Or, and here I want you to follow me carefully, cut them into little pieces and mail them back to their family! Now do you want that to happen to your favorite police chief or not?"

"No, I don't," said Brutus, sobered by this horrifying prospect, which seemed to come straight from the pages of a James Patterson novel.

"Well, then," she said. "Let's go. And make it snappy."

"But..."

"Do you *want* Uncle Alec to die a gruesome death? His body fed to the fishes?"

"Um, is this a trick question?" Brutus asked after a pregnant pause.

"Oh, for crying out loud. Up!" said Harriet, and gave her mate a shove against the rear.

"Easy, easy," said Brutus, as he defied gravity and raised himself up from the couch. "So where are we doing?"

"Out there into the world," said Harriet, vaguely gesturing to the great outdoors. "We're going to find traces and snoop clues, and we're going to find Uncle Alec and save him from certain death and a very painful and humiliating disfiguration."

And to show her cohort how it was done, she stuck her nose in the air and started sniffing.

☙

*G*ran had parked her car in front of Scarlett's apartment, and the latter now came hurrying out, carrying a bulky canvas shopping bag. She got into the car and dumped the bag on the backseat, right next to the two cats who, for some reason, were also present.

"What's with the cats?" she asked.

"They're going to help us find out what's going on," Vesta announced.

If Scarlett was surprised that cats were a fixture whenever Vesta was about to go on one of her adventures she didn't show it. It was part and parcel of being friends with the surprisingly spry septuagenarian. Wherever Vesta was, cats were never far away.

"So is that the stuff?" asked Vesta as she put the car in gear.

"Yeah, that's all of it. The guy at the store said it's pretty simple. All we need to do is conceal the bugs where Charlene won't find them, and they'll start transmitting their signal immediately. He did say we'd have to stay pretty close to pick up the signal."

"How close?"

"Within a hundred-foot radius."

"Bummer," said Vesta. "I don't feel like staying awake

twenty-four-seven to tail this woman until she gives up her many, many secrets."

"Which is why we should involve Wilbur and Francis," said Scarlett.

"No can do," said Vesta. "We've already got the cats involved, and I don't want Wilbur and Francis to know about my big secret."

Vesta's big secret was also her Achilles' heel. No one was supposed to know she could talk to her cats, and so far only Charlene and Scarlett knew about it, apart from Vesta's own family, of course.

"Why don't you simply tell them?" Scarlett suggested. "It would make life a lot easier."

"Yeah, tell Wilbur I can talk to cats. Before I finish telling him the whole town will know. You know what a gossip Wilbur Vickery is. The guy simply can't keep a secret."

"Yeah, that's true," Scarlett admitted. It was one of their fellow watch member's flaws. But also one of his strengths, since he was always *au courant* with the latest gossip.

"Besides, I don't want Charlene to know we're onto her. So Wilbur is out for Operation Mongoose."

"Operation Mongoose?" asked Scarlett with a laugh.

"It's as good a name as any," said Vesta with a shrug. "Now where do we go first?"

"Better start at the house," Scarlett suggested. "Then once we've got that bugged, we can take care of her office." How they were going to get access to the woman's phone was beyond her, though. They were no professional spies, after all. But somehow she figured Vesta would find a way around that minor disadvantage. She always did. "Does Charlene have an alarm system?"

"Nope. Alec told me he's been arguing with her to put one in and she turned him down flat. She says the moment she needs an alarm is the moment she's failed as a mayor and he's failed as chief of police. She still believes Hampton Cove is the kind of town where people should be able to leave their doors unlocked at all times."

"I'd love for things to be that way," said Scarlett wistfully.

"Me, too. Would make breaking in a lot easier for us."

10

I didn't mind assisting Gran and Scarlett on their quest to figure out why Gran's son was getting married to Charlene, but clearly she was laboring under a misapprehension that could very well impede the real investigation into Uncle Alec's disappearance.

So now Dooley and I were faced with what is commonly termed a dilemma: should we or shouldn't we tell these two what was really going on? Or follow Odelia's instructions and keep her grandmother in the dark?

"I think we should tell her," said Dooley. "She's Uncle Alec's mom. Mothers shouldn't be kept in the dark about their sons being kidnapped. To do so is morally ambiguous."

I smiled at my friend for using such a big word. I doubted whether he knew what it meant. "I think before we tell her we should probably ask Odelia. She clearly has her reasons and we don't want to go against her wishes."

Dooley made a face, showing me he was struggling with this as much as I was.

"And look at it this way: at least we'll be right at the heart of the investigation if we're going to be living with Charlene from now on."

"But what if these bad men come back? I'm not built for close-quarters combat, Max."

"Me, neither, Dooley," I admitted. "None of us are. So let's hope it doesn't come to that."

"I just wish Odelia didn't have to return Rambo to his owner," said Dooley now.

Rambo was a sizable Bulldog and a retired police dog, and had been instrumental in keeping us safe in a previous adventure. Odelia had wanted to adopt him, but Rambo already had an owner, who wasn't so keen to hand his aged dog over to someone else.

"If worse comes to worst, I'm sure Rambo's owner won't mind lending us his dog and his very particular skillset again," I said.

But until then? We were on our own, with only our smarts, wit and resourcefulness to carry us through. And the knowledge that the neighborhood watch was watching, of course. Though I wasn't exactly feeling reassured by that aspect of our mission.

Gran had pulled up outside Charlene Butterwick's home, and let us out of the car. The Mayor of Hampton Cove lived in a nice little home, though frankly I'd expected her to live in some villa or mansion. Then again, civil servants probably don't make the big bucks.

In front of her house plenty of flowers bloomed in a lovely little apron of green.

"Looks like your son's new wife got a green thumb," said Scarlett appreciatively.

"Mh," said Gran, regarding the floral display with a critical eye. "Not enough perennials. Her garden will look terrible come wintertime."

"Oh, don't be such a sourpuss," said Scarlett. "She's not

the worst possible daughter-in-law, is she now? In fact I think I remember you telling me not all that long ago how lucky Alec was to have found himself such a lovely lady as his new life partner."

"You must have misheard," said Gran, sticking her nose in the air and traipsing up to the door. She pressed her finger on the buzzer and inside the clanging echoed through the house. Patiently we waited on the doorstep, not exactly eager to start our mission, but not all that un-eager either, as we looked forward to launching into our investigation.

"Great," said Gran. "Nobody home. Let's do this, buddy."

And Dooley and I watched in confusion how our law-abiding human suddenly morphed into some kind of criminal mastermind and hopped it round the back, Dooley and myself in her wake, and then started messing around with the backdoor, applying what surely were illegal methods of gaining access!

"What is Gran doing, Max?" asked Dooley, as he watched on with surprise etched on his features.

"I think she's trying to break into Charlene's house," I replied, equally surprised.

It wasn't exactly the kind of scene a cat owner would want to subject their innocent pet to: Scarlett was holding up her phone, where a YouTube video was playing titled 'Breaking and Entering for Dummies,' while Vesta, her tongue sticking out of her mouth, was doing something with what looked like a toothpick and her Visa card.

"I can't watch this, Max," said Dooley, shaking his head.

"I know how you feel, Dooley," I said, though I was experiencing exactly the opposite: I simply couldn't look away from the scene!

"Can you play that last bit again?" asked Gran. "I think I missed something."

"Here, let me try," said Scarlett.

"No, it's fine," said Gran. "I can do this. I practiced at home and it worked just fine."

"Every lock is different, though, isn't it? I'm pretty sure your lock is different than this one."

"It's fine I'm telling you. I can do this. Just scroll back a couple of seconds."

With a sigh, Scarlett returned to an earlier moment in the video where the man, who looked like an ex-con, had shown what a lock looked like if you possessed X-ray vision.

"Why don't they just wait until Charlene gets home?" asked Dooley.

"I think they're going to plant those bugs now," I said. "They want to bug Charlene's entire house, remember? And her office, her phone and her car, too."

"This is not going to end well, Max."

"I have a feeling you're absolutely right, Dooley." Though who was going to arrest two old ladies when the Chief of Police himself had been kidnapped? The police force was effectively leaderless right now, even if it didn't know it yet.

"I think I heard a click," said Gran, pressing her ear against the lock.

"What kind of click?" asked Scarlett.

"How should I know? A click. Didn't he say something about a click?"

"Just let me try. You're doing it all wrong."

"No, I'm doing it exactly right!"

"He says first to insert that little metal thingy and then the other little metal thingy and wriggle!"

"I'm sure it's just the other way around."

"No, you've got it all wrong, Vesta, I'm telling you!"

"Get your hands away from me," said Vesta, slapping Scarlett's eager hands away.

"You have to put that there and that thing over there and then wiggle!"

"I'm wiggling my ass off here, all right? So if you just let me—"

And just when things were about to get physical, suddenly the door was opened and Charlene Butterwick appeared, looking at the two older ladies with a look of surprise.

"What's going on?" asked the Mayor, visibly taken aback by this surprising scene.

"We were just trying to ascertain if your security measures are on point," said Gran quickly, holding the tools of her burglarious trade behind her back where Scarlett equally quickly took them from her and dumped them into her purse. "Just one of the services your neighborhood watch likes to offer," she added with a beaming smile.

"It's what we do," Scarlett added. "We burglar-proof people's houses. Make sure they're safe."

Charlene still looked mildly suspicious, but finally nodded. "Thanks," she said. "So I guess your daughter and granddaughter decided to tell you what happened, huh?"

"Oh, sure," Gran lied. "They told us everything."

"If only I'd asked you to do this sooner," said Charlene as she stepped aside to invite both women into her home. "This could all probably have been prevented."

"Sure, sure," said Gran, and gestured for me and Dooley to follow her into the house. "And speaking of burglar-proofing your place, I've got the perfect gift for you, Charlene."

"What is it?" asked Charlene, who still looked extremely pale and drawn.

"I'm offering you my two cats," said Gran proudly, and pointed to Dooley and me, like a magician pulling a rabbit from a hat.

Charlene frowned. "I don't get it."

"Max and Dooley!" said Gran. "You can have them from

now on. They're two wonderful cats, house-trained and sweet-natured, and you can consider them an early wedding gift from me—"

"—and me!" Scarlett chimed in, displaying a wide smile that looked just a little unnatural, I thought. Or it could be that Scarlett never smiles, figuring it only adds to collagen loss and possible skin damage she can't afford at her age.

Charlene still wasn't fully on board, I could tell. "So... you're offering me your cats. Why, exactly?"

"Because... I want to welcome you into the family, honey," said Gran. "And what better way of welcoming you into the family than by offering you these two sweet fellas?"

"It's a Poole family tradition," Scarlett intimated, seeing how Gran was struggling and deciding to step in. "Whenever one of the Pooles gets married, cats exchange hands. It's the way things have always been done—isn't that right, Vesta?"

"Absolutely."

Charlene glanced down at Dooley and me, who just sat there looking as sweet as we could. And house-trained, of course, which was a given.

"But... I've never owned a cat in my life," said Charlene with a nervous little laugh. "I'm more of a dog person, really."

"That's all right," said Gran, waving a magnanimous hand. "We all make mistakes. Now are you just going to stand there or are you going to give them a big welcome? I don't hand my cats over to just anyone, you know. This is a big thing for me, Charlene."

"Oh, no, of course, of course," said Charlene, and crouched down next to me, then seemed at a loss at how exactly to proceed.

"Giving them a tickle behind the ears would be a good start," said Gran censoriously.

So Charlene gave me a tickle behind the ears and I dutifully purred. It wasn't a great tickle, mind you, but then cats can be great actors, so I just hammed it up a little: I dropped on the floor, rolled over like a dog, and even let her tickle my tummy.

Charlene smiled. "He's pretty sweet, isn't he?"

"Of course he is," said Gran. "Now do the other one. Get a feel for them."

And so Charlene repeated the procedure with Dooley, who mimicked my movements, and soon we were both lying on our backs for a tummy rub.

"I don't know about you, Max," said Dooley after a moment. "But I feel very silly."

"I know, Dooley," I said. "I feel very silly, too."

"Thanks, Vesta," said Charlene a little awkwardly. "Thank you so much."

And suddenly she burst into tears!

11

"So sweet of her to get so emotional over your gift," said Scarlett once they were back in the car.

"Yeah, I hadn't expected her to start blubbering like a baby," Vesta said. "But don't let that distract you from the mission, honey. She could very well have been playing us."

"Her tears looked real to me. And trust me, I know fake tears when I see them."

Vesta smiled. Scarlett knew what fake tears looked like because she'd probably employed the method herself on more than one occasion in the past, and knew how effective it was. "Did you manage to plant those bugs?"

"Yeah, I put one behind the bed, one behind the toilet and one in her home office."

"I distributed the rest around the living room," said Vesta. "So we should be good."

"Let's give it a test run," said Scarlett, sounding upbeat and happy after a successful mission pulled off without a hitch.

And as Vesta steered the car in the direction of Town Hall, Scarlett fiddled with her tablet for a moment, then suddenly Charlene's voice sounded through the car loud and clear.

"I don't have cat kibble for you guys," the Mayor was saying, "but I do have some turkey. Do you eat turkey?"

"Does a fish swim in the ocean?" grunted Vesta. "She really doesn't know the first thing about cats, does she?"

"What are you going to tell her when you take Max and Dooley out of there again?"

"I'll make something up. Maybe tell her I miss my babies too much and I underestimated how important they are to me."

"I think we did a pretty good job back there, pardner," said Scarlett, and held up her hand for a high-five.

"Damn near perfect job, pardner," said Vesta, and reciprocated the high-five with a high-five of her own. "Except for the lock picking. I feel like we should practice some more."

"And here is the perfect opportunity," said Scarlett as they entered the Town Hall parking lot and found themselves staring up at the modest one-story building.

"We better wait until it's dark," said Vesta. "Breaking into Charlene's house is one thing, but breaking into Town Hall is a different kettle of fish entirely." Especially since Town Hall, contrary to Charlene's home, was probably equipped with an alarm. Too bad her son wasn't answering his phone, or she could have asked him for the combination.

⁊♣

*C*harlene stared down at the two cats, who were both staring up at her intently, as if expecting her to do something, or to say something, or whatever.

"Um... so do you want me to take you guys for a walk?" she asked now. She was unsure of how to proceed. She hadn't lied when she'd told Vesta that she was a dog person.

49

She and Alec had recently even opened a dog kennel in town, though in actual fact it was an animal shelter where all pets were welcome, whether great or small, canine or otherwise inclined. She wondered if she should call the manager of the shelter and ask her for some tips and tricks on how to deal with cats, but then decided against it.

How hard could it be to care for these cuddly creatures? And they were so sweet, too.

Though the way they were staring at her, their gaze unwavering, their eyes never moving away from hers for even a second, was frankly making her feel a little uneasy.

"So, um... how do you guys feel about suddenly being donated to a new human? A little weird, right, this Poole family ritual?" She'd known that the Pooles had this thing about cats, but this whole thing about giving away cats to new partners entering the family was something she'd never heard of before. Alec hadn't mentioned it either.

"Look, if you guys expect me to talk to you, I'm very sorry but I can't. I don't speak your language, I'm afraid," she said when they just kept staring at her, not moving a muscle and not saying a single thing.

"So, um... just make yourselves comfortable, and I'll go and get you some food and, um..." And as the biggest of the twosome, the cat named Max, smacked his lips a little, she swallowed uncomfortably and quickly turned away. Oh, how she wished Alec was there.

❧

"She seems nice enough," said Dooley.

"Yeah, she's great," I said.

"Nervous, though. And unhappy."

"What do you expect, Dooley? Her boyfriend just got kidnapped before her eyes and who knows what these maniacs are up to next?" I sighed and glanced around. I already missed my favorite spot on Odelia's couch, and I knew I wasn't going to be able to sleep as soundly as I usually did. Not to mention the fact that Charlene probably had never heard of the words 'litter box,' something Gran conveniently forgot to mention.

"I think we'll have to do doo-doo and wee-wee in the backyard, Max," said Dooley, who'd noticed the same thing.

"Yeah, looks like it," I said. Which posed another problem: no pet flap!

Grandma Muffin had definitely done it this time. Giving us away? That hadn't been part of the deal. Did this mean we'd have to stay with Charlene forever? I didn't think I liked that. She was nice enough, sure, but even cats get attached to their own humans.

"Do you think we'll have to stay here forever now, Max?" asked Dooley as he glanced around. The living room was minimalistically furnished, all black and white, the entire house constructed in plenty of steel and glass. Not exactly the coziest environment I'd ever encountered, as it lent the place more of an office feel than a real home.

"I hope not," I said.

"I think Odelia won't be happy when she finds out that Gran has given us away to Charlene," Dooley surmised.

"And it's not as if she can take us back either," I said. "It's hard to take a gift back once you've given it. Especially a wedding gift."

"I never thought I'd be a wedding gift, Max."

"Me neither, Dooley."

But when Charlene returned from the kitchen carrying two porcelain plates heaped high with pieces of turkey, I quickly perked up. So maybe this new human of ours wasn't so bad after all? We'd just have to break her in, like cats do with all of their humans.

delia glanced around and frowned. "Have you seen the cats?" she asked.

"Didn't your grandmother take them?" said Chase. He was on the couch surfing on his laptop, busily going through a list of convicts Uncle Alec had collared. It was a long list.

"Yeah, but they should have been back by now," she said. "Unless she took them along on one of her neighborhood watch patrols."

"Then that must be it. You know how she loves those patrols."

Odelia hadn't seen any sign of Harriet and Brutus either, but then they spent most of their time next door, at her parents' place.

She decided to wander over there. She needed to talk to her mother anyway. But when she entered her parents' kitchen, neither her mother or her father were in evidence, and of the cats there was no trace either.

Weird. People just kept disappearing, though of course the case of her uncle being kidnapped had everyone on edge, so things weren't exactly normal right now.

And as she walked out again, she noticed a flyer her mom or dad had put up on the fridge with magnets. She read it with a rising sense of surprise.

'Madame Solange will tell you everything you need to know about your future. Schedule a consult now, and find out what the future holds in store for you and your nearest and dearest.'

There was a phone number, and someone had circled it twice, adding a few exclamation marks for good measure.

And just as she was about to walk out of the house, her dad came walking in, his hands laden with bags of groceries, followed by Odelia's mom, likewise occupied.

"I'm sorry, honey," said Mom. "Did you want us to get something for you?"

"No, we're fine," said Odelia, who'd forgotten it was grocery run day. In spite of her uncle having gone missing, life still went on, of course, and people still had to eat.

"What's with this Madame Solange thing?" she asked as she idly checked the bags. She'd skipped dinner, as the emergency meeting with Charlene had run late, and then she hadn't felt like eating and neither had Chase.

"Oh, just something I picked up at the supermarket," said her mother, waving a dismissive hand.

"So did you call the number?" she asked.

"Mh? Oh, no, of course not. You know I don't believe in that kind of stuff, honey. And neither does your father."

"What stuff?" asked her dad, breezing into the kitchen again.

"Fortune telling stuff," said Mom with a careless laugh that sounded a little forced.

"Baloney," said her dad sternly. "Every last one of those people should be sued for taking advantage of the naivety of their victims."

"I wouldn't go as far as that," protested her mother as she put the groceries in the fridge, while Dad offered the same courtesy to the pantry. "I'll bet some of them are the real deal —the genuine article. Though I still have to meet the first one who can actually predict the future," she hurriedly added.

"So this Solange, where can I find her?" asked Odelia, her mom's behavior making her curious to find out more. It was the reporter in her. She could never leave well enough alone.

Mom swallowed. "I'm not sure. I don't think she's from around here."

"I thought you said you hadn't called her?"

"Oh, but I didn't! I would never spend money on that sort of thing."

"So how do you know she's not from around here?"

Her mom shrugged. "Just a wild guess. If she were from around here, we'd have heard of her by now, don't you think? Or you would have written an article about her."

"Maybe I will," said Odelia, and studied her mother's reaction carefully.

Mom didn't disappoint her. She looked up in alarm. "You're going to talk to her?"

"I might," said Odelia, now absolutely sure her mom was hiding something, which made her want to pursue the matter even more. "I'll bet there's a great story there."

"Oh, no!" said her mother quickly. "I'm sure nobody wants to read about fortune tellers. That kind of thing is so passé."

"I'll bet she's down at the fair," said her dad now.

"There's a fair in town?" asked Odelia.

"Oh, sure. They've been setting up for the past couple of days. I think they'll do a big parade through town any day now, though I'm afraid carnivals and fairgrounds and circuses are becoming a thing of the past. People aren't into that kind of thing anymore nowadays. They prefer their entertainment more… hip and cool." He grinned at his daughter as he said it, indicating he was anything but hip or cool.

"Look, who cares about this fair, or Madame Solange?" said Mom, taking a seat at the kitchen table. "What are we going to do about my brother? What do you propose?"

"Chase is working on it," said Odelia, sobering. "He's looking through a list of the people Uncle Alec put behind bars and who recently were released, as you suggested."

"So the police are going to handle it? Even though these kidnappers specifically warned Charlene not to get them involved?"

"Chase is not working the case as a cop. He's working it as a member of this family," said Odelia. "Though frankly I think we actually *should* involve the police. I think that's what Uncle Alec would want."

"I hope they don't hurt him," said Mom. "And why did they make Charlene announce their wedding? That just doesn't make any sense."

"I'll bet it's some kind of psychological thing," said Dad as he leaned against the kitchen wall, looking pensive. "Psychological warfare. To make Charlene crack."

"How is announcing her wedding going to make Charlene crack?" asked Mom pointedly.

"I don't know," said her dad with a shrug. "But it smells a lot like psychological warfare to me." And he disappeared into the living room.

"Oh, your father with his nonsense explanations," said Mom. "I didn't even want to go shopping. How can we pretend life is normal when my brother is somewhere out there, suffering who knows what kinds of torments?" Tears had formed in her eyes, and Odelia took her mother's hands and gave them a reassuring squeeze.

"We'll find him, Mom," she said. "Chase is the best at what he does, and I'm not too shabby either."

"And what happened to our cats?" asked Mom. "I haven't seen them anywhere—I just hope they haven't been taken, too."

13

"So, um, you guys?" said Charlene.

Dooley and I looked up. We'd eaten our fill in exquisitely tasty turkey, and our new owner had made us a cozy little spot on the couch by placing down an actual down blanket for us to lie on, and had turned the TV to a channel that showed plenty of cat food commercials. So when she called us, we knew we were in for more treats.

"Let's go,'" said Charlene now. She looked and sounded a little subdued, I thought, but then that was to be expected, since her future husband had been rudely taken from her.

"She's holding something in her hand, Max," said Dooley. "Are those... dog leashes?"

"I think so," I said, wincing a little.

"Let's take you guys for a walk," said Charlene. Bless her heart, she was trying hard to turn herself into a proper cat lady, but dog leashes? And taking us for a walk? Clearly she had no idea what she was doing.

"Let's just humor her," I said with a shrug.

"But I don't like a leash, Max. It makes me feel so... like a dog."

"I know, Dooley, but clearly Charlene isn't herself today, and I think we should indulge her."

So we both jumped down from the couch and walked up to our new human.

"Let's try these on for size," said the Mayor. "I think they should fit you just fine."

And they did. They fit exactly right, but that didn't mean I liked the sensation of a leash being attached to my collar.

At least she hadn't removed our collars, though thus far there wasn't all that much for Gran and Scarlett to learn from keeping tabs on Charlene.

"You know the drill," said Charlene. "We'll go for a walk around the block, and if you feel the need to do your business, please do it against a tree." She quickly inspected the pockets of her cardigan. "Poo baggies—check. Tissue paper—check. I think I'm ready to take my new cats for a walk for the very first time. Are you guys ready?"

"Yes, Charlene," I said dutifully.

"Yes, Charlene," Dooley chimed in.

Charlene smiled. "So weird," she muttered, and then walked out of the house, but not before taking a quick glance through the window to see if there weren't any more of those home invasion people lurking about. "I probably should hire myself some protection," she said now, talking to herself more than to us. "I'll call a security company first thing in the morning. I don't even feel safe in my own home, that's the worst part. And I can't stop thinking about poor Alec. He must be going through hell right now."

"I'm sure Uncle Alec will be fine, Charlene," I assured her as we walked down the gravel path that split her front yard and through the little gate and out onto the sidewalk. "He's a police chief, after all, so he's probably used to dealing with the scum of the earth."

"Maybe he's managed to escape already," said Dooley, "and he's on his way home as we speak."

"Yeah, I'm sure Dooley is right," I said. "Uncle Alec will probably be home soon, and then he'll put all of those nasty home invasion people in prison where they belong."

But of course Charlene couldn't understand a word we said, poor thing, so our comforting speech fell on deaf ears.

We walked around the block, and I have to admit it wasn't as bad as I thought. Of course cats aren't used to being walked like a dog, but that bit of fresh air was doing me the world of good after having been cooped up inside the house all evening, and frankly I did feel the need to do a little doo-doo and a little wee-wee, and so did Dooley.

And so we gave Charlene quite a bit of work cleaning up after us. I would have done it myself, but it's tough digging a hole in the sidewalk, just as it was tough for me to have to deposit it there. Then again, I didn't have a choice in the matter, and neither did Dooley.

And we'd walked probably half a block when suddenly we saw a parade of some kind heading our way. There were a lot of cars and trailers, fancifully painted in bright colors, and I could even see an elephant walking along, and a cage containing an actual lion!

"Hey, look. It's one of our relatives," I told Dooley.

More people had come out of their houses, leaving their televisions to watch the spectacle that was being announced by a sort of carnival barker riding on top of the elephant.

"Hey, cousin!" I said, waving at the lion. But he either couldn't hear me, or wasn't interested in making my acquaintance, for he totally ignored me.

Clowns were also there, and jugglers, and what looked like trapeze artists, judging from their Spandex outfits, though they'd left their nice and trusty trapezes at home.

"Alec and I went there yesterday," said Charlene now. "It was wonderful." She gave a wistful sigh, clearly thinking about those halcyon days of yore. "The fair will be there for another two weeks or so and then they'll move on to the next town."

"Charlene talks to herself a lot, doesn't she?" said Dooley.

"I think it soothes her," I said. "It makes her feel less anxious about what happened to Uncle Alec."

So maybe it had been a good idea for Gran to give us to Charlene as a present, even though her intentions had been less therapeutic and more born from deep suspicion.

One of the final trailers in the parade had the words 'Madame Solange' painted across the side, and up in front sat a woman dressed in a sort of flowing robe. She looked to be in her early thirties, had long fair hair with two small braids, and was really pretty.

And oddly enough, next to the woman sat a man, who looked like the spitting image of... Uncle Alec!

Charlene must have seen it, too, for she did a double take, then said, "Isn't that Alec over there?" And then without awaiting our response—and why would she?—she started frantically waving at the man, who sat stoically staring before him.

Madame Solange, who must have thought Charlene was waving at her, returned the wave with a vague smile on her pretty face.

But then Charlene was yanking us forward and in the direction of the trailer.

"Alec!" she yelled. "Alec, it's me!"

But this Alec lookalike didn't even look up at the sudden commotion.

And then, before Charlene could reach Madame Solange's trailer, suddenly a couple of burly men showed up, and physically held her back. They must have been parade security, protecting the fair and circus people from overzealous fans like Charlene.

And as Charlene kept jogging alongside the trailer, dragging us along with her, I noticed something else. Cameras! Everywhere I looked I saw cameras filming the parade, and now also filming the crazy woman dragging two poor cats and yelling 'Alec' all the while.

"Please, ma'am," said one of the security people. "For your own safety, please stay behind the barrier."

"But that's my boyfriend up there!" said Charlene.

"Where?" asked the burly man, giving her a look of confusion.

"Up there with that woman. His name is Alec and he's my boyfriend."

"That's impossible, ma'am," said the security guy. "That's Wolf, Madame Solange's husband. And now I'm going to have to ask you to please return behind the barrier."

So Charlene did as she was told, even though clearly she wasn't happy about it.

And it has to be said, the guy only shared a vague resemblance to Uncle Alec. For one thing, this Wolf sported a funky rust-colored mustache. And for another, he had a full head of hair, something Uncle Alec hadn't been able to claim for many, many years.

"Poor Charlene," said Dooley. "Now she's starting to see things."

"It's normal," I said. "She'll start seeing Uncle Alec everywhere she goes from now on. It's the strain from the kidnapping that's starting to make itself felt now."

"I really thought it was him," our new human now murmured softly. "Sweet Alec…"

And then she started the trek home, and frankly not a

moment too soon, too. People were starting to point at her, and those camera crews that had captured her frantic intervention would probably be transmitting that footage of a mayor gone berserk.

If Charlene wasn't careful, soon she would be mayor of Hampton Cove no more.

14

*M*arge compared the numbers on her lottery ticket with the ones on the television screen and had to admit they didn't match—not one single number had she gotten right.

Disappointed, she crumpled up the ticket and thought dark thoughts of that woman—that Madame Solange, who'd promised she'd win the lottery in the next couple of days.

Three days had gone by since she and Tex visited the fortune teller at the fair and still nothing. So far she'd only lost money, not gained a single cent, and Tex's prediction hadn't materialized either.

"Better luck next time, hon," said her husband, rubbing her back consolingly.

"Yeah, I wouldn't be too sure about that," she said.

"If Madame Solange said you're going to win, you're going to win. I'm sure about it."

"I think Odelia is on to us," said Marge as she darted a quick look at the family room door. Odelia had a habit of dropping by unannounced. That was the disadvantage of having a professional reporter for a daughter: snooping around and listening at keyholes came naturally to this breed of nosy parkers, even when it concerned their own family.

"I think I made a convincing case though, didn't I?" Tex said.

"Oh, yeah, I thought you were great, honey. She'd never think you were as keen on Madame Solange as I am." Though her excitement was waning fast.

Just then, there was a rattle of the mailbox, and she frowned. The postwoman never came by this late. But since her favorite show was about to start, it was up to Tex to take a look. When he returned, he just stood there, frowning at a piece of paper in his hand.

"What were those winning lottery numbers again, honey?" he asked.

"Um… Five, four, and the rest I don't remember."

His shoulders sagged. "Nope. I thought for a moment…" And he walked over to place a lottery ticket into her hands.

She stared at it, then frowned as recognition dawned. "I think those are the winning numbers from two days ago," she said slowly. She locked eyes with her husband, and then they were both frantically grabbing for their phones to look up the numbers.

"You're right!" said Tex, a little quicker off the mark than her. "You're absolutely right!"

"How much?" she asked. "How much did we win?"

"Fifty thousand, it says here," said her husband, slowly looking up at her, then down at the ticket lying in her lap.

"Fifty thousand? But…"

"I don't get it," he said, taking a closer look at the envelope the ticket had arrived in. It was just a blank envelope, with nothing written on it. "How can this be?"

"Who cares?" said Marge, a smile slowly lighting up her face. "Madame Solange was right: we won the lottery, Tex! We won!"

"Yoo-hoo! Finally!"

And then they were both getting up and hugging it out before Marge realized being happy and celebrating their lottery success, no matter how strangely it had come about, was inappropriate with her brother still missing.

Suddenly the doorbell rang, and they first looked at each other, then in the direction of the door. This time they both walked the short distance to open it, and they found a thickset cameraman standing before them, and an excited-looking young reporter with purple-framed glasses and a yellow goatee sticking a microphone under their noses.

"WLBC-9—your best source of local news! Tex and Marge Poole?"

Tex and Marge nodded dumbly.

"I apologize for the intrusion," said the guy, "but I believe you're both familiar with a person named Madame Solange?"

Once more, Tex and Marge nodded dumbly.

"I'd like to ask you a couple of questions. But first, the most important one: did you or didn't you recently win the lottery?"

"We did," said Marge, finally finding her voice.

"We just found out," added Tex.

"Wonderful! Amazing! Great! You will remember that your visit to Madame Solange a couple of days ago was being taped, right?"

Vaguely Marge remembered that Madame Solange had warned them the consult was being recorded. She hadn't minded, figuring it was probably some security thing.

"We've been following Madame Solange around for the past six months, all part of a series on fortune tellers and paranormal phenomena, and as a follow-up we also like to talk to the people whose fortunes she predicted. People like you, Marge and Tex Poole."

"Okay," said Marge, understanding dawning. "So you

want to see how accurate Madame Solange's predications are, is that it?"

"Exactly! So tell us, Marge Poole, how much did Madame Solange predict you'd win?"

"She didn't give us a specific number, but she did say it would be a hefty sum."

"And how much did you win?"

"Fifty thousand," said Tex with a big smile, and showed the camera crew the winning lottery ticket in question.

"And as far as your prediction goes, Tex Poole, what did Madame Solange tell you?"

"She said I'd go on a Caribbean cruise," said Tex, his smile fading a little.

"And have you made plans in that direction?" asked the reporter.

"Not yet," said Tex, then glanced down at the lottery ticket, then at his wife, and his smile returned in full force. "But I guess now we can finally take that cruise we've been talking about, honey!"

"Oh, my God!" said Marge. "Of course!"

"Oo-wee!" said the reporter. "Looks like Madame Solange was right on the... money!"

Marge would have told the guy that the ticket had magically appeared in their mailbox, but in the face of their big win that seemed like such a minor detail now. And since it would only detract from the bigger picture, which was that they'd won a big bundle of cash, and were finally going on that cruise, she decided not to bother.

Madame Solange had been right. Twice! That was the main takeaway here.

15

---

*H*arriet and Brutus had been wandering through town, and had finally arrived at their destination: the house where Charlene Butterwick lived.

"So this is the place, huh?" said Brutus, panting a little. It had been a long walk, and his paws were hurting.

"Yep, this is it," said Harriet. "So let's start hunting around for clues, snuggle pooh. I'm pretty sure these kidnappers must have left some."

Brutus would have reminded Harriet that clues weren't like breadcrumbs: you couldn't just strew them around here and there, but felt that Harriet was right in another regard: surely these kidnappers had been seen by someone? So what they needed to do now was find these someones and grill them for information until they cracked.

"Let's go talk to that big guy over there," Harriet suggested, and pointed to a very large canine who stood barking at them from behind a fence.

Brutus, who disliked dogs as much as the next cat, wasn't all that keen on making this particular dog's acquaintance, but then again, a clue was a clue, and they needed to find Uncle Alec, didn't they?

So they both traipsed across the street and joined the large dog, who was yapping even louder now that two cats looked like they were about to invade his territory.

"Cool it, buddy," said Harriet. "All we want is some information."

"No way are you setting paw in here," said the dog in response. He was a big brown dog, and if Brutus wasn't mistaken belonged to the Danish Dog variety.

"What makes you think we're even remotely interested in setting paw in there?" asked Harriet. "We have our own homes, dog, so you can keep yours, all right?"

"Oh," said the dog, not expecting this comeback. "So what do you want, exactly?"

"A crime was committed across the street," said Harriet. "A man was kidnapped, and we were wondering if you saw something."

"Yeah, I saw something," said the dog, giving Harriet a curious look. It probably wasn't every day that cats came inquiring after kidnapped people. "So what's it to you?"

"That man is our human's brother," said Brutus, "and she would like to get him back before these bad men hurt him beyond repair."

"Well said, Brutus," said Harriet. "So how about it? What can you tell us?"

The dog sank down on his haunches and gave them a sly look. "What's in it for me?"

"The satisfaction of having solved a crime, that's what," said Harriet, and it was immediately clear the dog wasn't all that happy with her answer, for he made a face.

"I'm not into solving crime, cat, so I don't really care if you find your human or not."

Harriet cocked her head. "You don't care if Alec Lip is

found? Chief of police and the person in charge of the police station?"

"Nope. I don't care one bit," said the dog, and yawned cavernously to show them exactly how little he cared about Uncle Alec's fate.

"You do know that the chief of police in this town is also in charge of the rules and regulations governing the use of our parks and sidewalks, don't you? And so far I think Chief Alec has been very lenient when it comes to dogs being able to do their business both on those same sidewalks and in those same parks. But what if I tell you his second-in-command, Chase Kingsley, who now stands to take over, takes a much harder line?"

"He does?" asked the dog, showing signs of concern.

"Oh, sure. Chase Kingsley hates dogs with a vengeance. He was once bitten by a dog, you see, and he's made it his mission in life to make your lives as miserable as he can."

The dog glanced at Brutus, who nodded solemnly. "You're in for a very bumpy ride, buddy."

"What do you mean?"

"I'm talking about the new ordinance forbidding dogs to be walked," said Harriet. "Forcing their owners to make them do their business in litter boxes from now on. So no more walks in the park for you, sir. No more refreshing rambles along the sidewalks and the roads of our town. And most importantly no more walks along the beach."

"No more walks along the beach!"

"Oh, for sure. You'll be cooped up inside for the rest of your natural life, Mr…"

"Buddy," said Buddy sadly.

"No more running wild and free. No more doing your business al fresco. No more—"

"All right, all right! I get your point! What do you want?"

"If we can find Chief Alec, and he's reinstated as Chief of

Police, Kingsley won't be able to carry through his frankly apocalyptic plans, and your life will go on the way it always has. So are you going to help us find Chief Alec or do you prefer Kingsley to be the new chief?"

"No! Please not Chief Kingsley! I like to run along the beach, and I love to do my business al fresco! I'll tell you everything I know!"

Harriet gave her friend and partner a cheeky wink and he grinned. Harriet would have made a great police cat.

"So tell us what you saw."

"Three guys, heavily built, all wearing masks when they came out of the house. But then one took off his mask, and he had a shaven head, cause it reflected the light from that lamplight over there. He looked like a real tough guy, with a crooked nose and a jutting chin. He also had cauliflower ears."

"Excellent powers of observation, Buddy," said Brutus appreciatively.

"Thanks. The nights get pretty lonely out here, so I like to spend them people watching."

"Anything else?" asked Harriet.

"Well, they came out with a fourth guy, who didn't seem to like what was going on, for he kept struggling. He had a hood over his head, and his hands were tied behind his back."

"That was Chief Alec," said Brutus.

"They put him in a panel van and drove off, and that's all I know."

"Did you catch the license plate?" asked Harriet.

"Lady, I'm not a cop, all right? I don't care about license plates, unless my owner gives me one I can chew on. All I know is that the van was the same type of van my owner's got. An old Ford van. Looks like a big box on wheels?"

"Color?"

"Dark green. And did I say it was an old model? You

should have heard the racket that thing was making, and the fumes spewing from that exhaust!" He shook his head. "They should probably have that looked at."

"I'll tell them when I see them," said Harriet laconically. "Well, Buddy," she said, holding out a paw. "Thank you so much for the information."

Buddy tapped her paw, then tapped Brutus's paw, and said, "For a pair of cats you guys ain't half bad."

"And for a dog you ain't so bad either," Harriet said with a smile.

Buddy laughed. "Wait till I tell the boys that I saved their lives by helping out a couple of cats! They'll never believe me!"

And as they turned away from Buddy, they almost bumped into... Max and Dooley, tied to leashes, and being walked by... Charlene Butterwick!

16

I was more than a little surprised when we returned from our walk and saw none other than Harriet and Brutus suddenly showing up.

"What are you doing here?" asked Harriet.

"What are *you* doing here?" I countered.

"Hey, aren't you the rest of Odelia's cats?" asked Charlene, who'd also spotted the new arrivals.

"Gran gave us to Charlene as a present," said Dooley sadly. "We belong to Charlene now, me and Max."

"Are those… leashes?" asked Brutus, staring at the strange contraptions.

"And… collars?" asked Harriet.

I could have sunk through the pavement from sheer embarrassment. It's never a pleasant experience for a cat to be seen wearing a collar, or, God forbid, a dog leash, and so I reluctantly acknowledged the fact. "Charlene isn't familiar with cats," I said. "She thinks we have to be walked two or three times a day, like dogs, hence the leashes."

"And Gran has given us these collars," Dooley explained. "She put bugs in them, though they don't bite."

"Bugs as in electronic listening devices," I clarified. "She wants to listen in on Charlene, still thinking she somehow tricked Uncle Alec into marriage."

"She put the house full of bugs, too," said Dooley, "but she assured us they're not the kind of bugs that will multiply like crazy and make us sick."

"Wow," said Harriet. "And here we thought Gran had chosen you for some cushy job. And all the while you're more to be pitied than envied, I must say."

"Yeah, but at least we got fed turkey," I said a little defensively. "So there's that."

"And there's plenty more where that came from," added Dooley.

Harriet and Brutus shared a look. "I like turkey," said Harriet.

"I *love* turkey," said Brutus.

And both directed a very obvious but very effective pleading look at Charlene, who now smiled and said, "I think I'll take you guys inside with me. You missed your friends, didn't you? Of course you did."

I could have told her that cats are solitary creatures who only very rarely miss their friends, but I had to admit she had a point. I had thought about what life would be like without Harriet and Brutus from now on, and it had seemed a little bleak, to be honest.

So the four of us followed the Mayor into her home, and before long we were all snacking on that delicious turkey meat, that must have cost her an arm and a leg.

"I think I know what happened to Uncle Alec," said Harriet between two bites of the delicacy. "Buddy from across the street saw the men that took him. He says one of them had a shaven head and cauliflower ears, and they were driving an old dark green Ford van with a busted exhaust pipe. He didn't catch the license plate but now I'm thinking:

how many dark green Ford vans can there possibly be driving on these streets, right?"

"We have to tell Chase," I said.

Only problem was: how were we ever going to talk to Chase now that we were pretty much locked up inside Charlene's home?

"Oh, and Charlene thinks she saw Uncle Alec," said Dooley. "Only it wasn't Uncle Alec but someone who looked just like him but with more hair. His real name is Wolf and he was riding on a trailer next to his wife, a woman named Madame Solange."

"Marge and Tex visited someone called Madame Solange a couple of days ago," said Harriet. "They were pretty excited when they got home. Couldn't stop talking about it."

"This Solange promised they'd win the lottery," said Brutus.

"And a Caribbean cruise," said Harriet.

"So she's a fortune teller," I said with a shrug.

"What's a fortune teller, Max?" asked Dooley.

"It's a woman who can tell you about your future," I said. "Though I'm not sure it's not just a trick."

"This Madame Solange can tell us about our future?" he asked, looking up from his close inspection of the substance on his porcelain plate.

"That's what she claims, anyway."

"Maybe we should go and talk to her. I would like to know about my future."

"I wouldn't," said Brutus. "What if she predicts something bad? I don't want to know something bad is going to happen to me."

"I think I'd want to know if something bad will happen," Harriet mused. "That way I can make sure it doesn't happen."

"Oh, it will happen," said Brutus, "and not much you can do about it."

"No, but what if she predicts, like, that I'll be run over by a truck on April the 14th at three o'clock in the afternoon? All I have to do is stay home that day, and I'll be fine."

"It'll happen some other day," Brutus said. "You can't cheat death, Harriet. It'll find a way to make that prediction come true. So it's better not to know, so you don't worry."

"I still say we pay a visit to this Madame Solange," said Harriet stubbornly.

"So I've made the bed in the guest room for you guys," said Charlene. "I hope that suits you. I'm sorry, but I have no idea how to take care of four cats," she added, and then abruptly disappeared again.

"She seems a little frazzled," said Harriet.

"Completely out of it," said Brutus, shaking his head.

"That's only to be expected after what she went through," I said. "I think she should probably go and see a shrink."

"What does a shrink do, Max?" asked Dooley.

"They shrink people's heads," said Brutus with a grin. "So their heads don't bother them so much anymore."

Dooley stared at him. "Shrink their heads! But how?"

"Well, shrinks have special machines that turn people's heads the size of a peanut."

"Oh, no!"

"Don't listen to him, Dooley," I said. "A shrink is a person who digs deep into a person's psyche and tries to help them come to terms with certain traumatic experiences, like their boyfriends being snatched right from under their noses."

"Oh," said Dooley, nodding, and gave Brutus a slightly offended look, which the latter totally ignored.

"That was great, you guys," said Harriet. "But now I'm afraid Brutus and I have to get going. We need to tell Chase what we discovered, so he can find Uncle Alec."

And so she and Brutus walked over to the front door,

only to discover that it missed one very important addition: a pet flap.

So they moved over to the back door, which was a sliding glass door, just like the one Odelia has, but of course there was no pet flap there either. And when they both started whining, and then started scratching the glass to be let out, Charlene merely said, "Oh, how cute!" and went about her business without bothering to open the door.

She probably thought this was normal behavior for cats.

And so we were all locked in there with a slightly loopy Mayor—possibly for eternity!

17

"So what do you hear?" asked Scarlett.

Vesta, who was frowning and listening intently, said, "Shush!" then listened some more. "I hear exactly nothing! Nothing!" she said finally, and took off her earphones. "Are you sure this stuff works?"

"The guy at the store said it works just fine. You plant the bugs, then you download the app, and you listen! How hard can it be?"

"Huh," said Vesta, and picked up the brochure Scarlett had gotten when she bought the surveillance equipment. She leafed through it. "So... you put the batteries in, right?"

"Oh, sure. The guy at the store put in all the batteries."

"So did you turn them on?" When Scarlett didn't respond, Vesta glanced over to her friend. "You did turn on the bugs, right?"

"Um..." said Scarlett, studying a long fingernail.

"Oh, Scarlett!"

"I forgot, okay!"

"I turned on mine, and we know they work, because we

got a clear signal from them before, which means we can only hear Charlene when she's downstairs in the living room." She gave her friend a hard look. "So no feed from the bedroom, the bathroom, or Charlene's home office—that's just great!"

"Look, I'm not a professional bug person, okay? If you wanted a professional bug person you should have asked your granddaughter to tag along."

"Odelia probably doesn't know the first thing about bugs either," Vesta grunted.

"Who does?!"

"Okay, so this is not a problem. We simply go back in there tomorrow and turn on all of the bugs *you* planted." She hadn't mentioned this to Scarlett, but unfortunately she herself had completely forgotten to turn on the bugs she planted on the cats, too! Aargh!

"And what are you going to tell Charlene? We forgot to turn on our listening devices so just give us a minute and we'll go and do that now?"

"No, you just lure her into the backyard with some excuse while I check on the bugs. And at least now we know we need to double-check the bugs we plant at Town Hall."

"Fine. So when do you want to do this?"

"We better do it now. I'm getting tired of sitting in this damn car."

They'd returned from Town Hall to sit in front of Charlene's house for a while, hoping to get the goods on the Mayor, but the bug fiasco had thrown a spanner in the works. First they'd heard the woman loud and clear, but probably she'd retired to bed, and since Scarlett hadn't turned on the bugs upstairs—end of broadcast! The two elderly wannabe spies had already ordered pizza, delivered to the car by a pizza delivery kid who gave them funny looks, and they'd also ordered a big meal from a Chinese food

78

delivery guy, who'd given them even funnier looks. Their sanitary needs had been taken care of by using a local park, where they'd ducked behind some bushes to do their business.

All in all this whole spy business was a lot less glamorous than it was on TV!

And since there was nothing more to be gleaned from staking out Charlene's house, Vesta drove them across town and parked in front of Town Hall once more. This time all was dark inside, and so the time for some action-packed shenanigans had finally arrived!

"Okay, let's do this!" said Scarlett, and when Vesta didn't move, she frowned. "What is it? Having second thoughts?"

"No, I'm just wondering why my son still hasn't returned any of my calls."

They'd even walked over to the police station before to catch him in his office but he hadn't been behind his desk, and when they'd asked Dolores where the Chief was, the dispatcher-slash-receptionist had said she had no clue, which was pretty weird.

Almost as if Alec had simply... disappeared.

"You don't think Charlene killed him, do you?" asked Scarlett now.

"I don't know, but I wouldn't put it past her. She's like one of those Praying Mantises: the ones that kill their mate once they've squeezed all the juice out of them."

"Ugh. Please don't talk about your son's juice, Vesta. It's gross."

"It's just a metaphor!"

"Even so, it's gross." They both sat there for a moment, then Scarlett said, "When we pay another visit to Charlene tomorrow we need to search that place top to bottom. If she did kill your son, we need to find him so we have proof."

"I know," said Vesta, the thought of her son having been

murdered by this Praying Mantis Mayor weighing heavy on her.

"Because if we don't have proof, she'll simply pretend nothing happened, and we'll never be able to pin his murder on her."

"I know."

"She's a politician, and she'll get away with it."

"I know, okay?"

"I don't think you do, Vesta," said Scarlett, turning to her friend. "If she killed your son, and we find out, she'll come for us, too!"

Vesta gulped a little. "I knew she was bad news the minute I laid eyes on her."

"I thought you said she was the best thing that ever could have happened to Alec?"

"I never said that!"

"Fine. So let's go already, shall we? And let's search her office, too. She may have killed him in there and stashed his body underneath the floorboards."

"Oh, Christ," said Vesta, and they both got out of the car and quickly made their way over to Town hall, which was cloaked in darkness, only the front lit up by halogen lights.

They circled around to the back, and took a concrete staircase down into a recessed area that led to a metal door which gave access to a basement few people knew existed.

The metal door was locked tight, of course, but they'd anticipated this, and as Scarlett put on her protective mask, and so did Vesta, the latter took out the blowtorch Scarlett had bought earlier that day and started burning a big hole in that metal door.

So when five minutes later the night guard did his second tour of the night, and found two old ladies using a blowtorch to break into Town Hall, he immediately called for backup, then proceeded to point a very large gun at the two ladies before yelling, "Put your weapons down now! And put your hands where I can see them!"

And so it was that Scarlett Canyon and Vesta Muffin were being arrested for breaking and entering... again.

18

J was starting to get a little worried that we might never be able to escape Charlene's abode, but luckily I suddenly remembered that I needn't have worried: we were, after all, in contact with Gran at all times, through the bugs hidden in our collars!

So I simply said, "Gran, if you can hear me, I think now might be a good time to come and get us. Charlene is acting a little weird, and now Harriet and Brutus are also here with us, and they've found a great clue as to Uncle Alec's whereabouts."

Look, I know I said I wasn't going to tell Gran what had happened to her son, but necessity knows no law, and we couldn't simply keep this vital clue to ourselves when Uncle Alec's life was in danger and the clue could lead us to his kidnappers, could we?

"Gran?" said Dooley, also speaking into his collar. "Are you there?"

"This isn't a two-way bug, Dooley," I said. "Gran can hear us, but she can't talk to us."

"Oh," he said, looking disappointed. "But then how do we know if she's listening?"

"Of course she's listening," I said. "You don't think Gran would send us in here and leave us to our own devices, do you? She's listening right now, and hearing every word we say."

"Gran, we just want you to know that Brutus and I found the clue," said Harriet, speaking into my collar. "*We* did—not Max or Dooley. Just making that very clear."

"Yeah, we talked to Buddy and Buddy told us what happened," Brutus added for good measure. "And by us I obviously mean Harriet and myself—not Max and not Dooley."

"Okay, you don't have to rub it in," I said. "You found the clue, and so all the credit goes to you guys."

"Gran, did you get all that?" said Harriet. "Max has just admitted that Brutus and I are much, much smarter than he is."

"I didn't say that!" I cried.

"No, but you implied it."

"I did no such thing!"

"It did sound like that to me, Max," said Brutus, giving me an impish grin. "And I'm pretty sure it sounded like that to Gran, too. Isn't that right, Gran?!" he practically yelled into my collar.

"She's not deaf, Brutus," I said. "These bugs are highly sensitive gadgets and they pick up the minutest sound."

"I hope she's recording this. I want it on the record that Max said we're smarter than him," said Harriet.

"Oh, God," I groaned.

"So when is she going to come and get us, Max?" asked Dooley.

"Soon, Dooley," I said. "Very soon now."

Harriet checked the big clock over the kitchen counter.

"So she's only a couple of minutes away, right? And if she's hearing this now, she should be here in… ten?"

"Oh, that's great," said Dooley. "I didn't want to say this before? But I kinda miss home, you know. And I miss my own humans."

"Yeah, me, too, Dooley," I admitted. Charlene was nice and all, and she served us up some delicious food, on gorgeous plates, but life is about more than just food and a soft couch, or even a cozy guest bedroom. It's also about the humans you decide to share your life with, and Charlene was a great human, but she wasn't our human.

"Are you guys still up?" the Mayor said, popping her head from the bedroom to see what we were up to. "Don't you like the space I prepared for you?"

So we followed her into the spare bedroom and when we saw the nice bed she'd made for us, I felt bad that soon Gran would ring the front door and announce that she was taking us home again.

"Okay, so maybe we can stay a little while longer," I now announced to my collar. "Charlene looks like she could use the company. So please come and get us in the morning, Gran. But wait until we've had breakfast. This turkey really is something else."

And besides, we'd told Gran all about the great clues Harriet and Brutus had found, so it didn't really matter now if she came to find us or not.

And then Charlene looked so sad that instead of spending the night in the guest bedroom, we followed her into her own bedroom instead, and before long we were fast asleep on the Mayoral bed, the first time I'd ever slept in the presence of a VIP, I have to say.

*O*delia frowned and shook her head. "I don't get it. They never take off like this. Never."

"I know, babe. Have you tried your Gran's phone?"

"Yeah, she's not picking up."

They were in the bedroom, but Odelia couldn't sleep, as she hadn't seen her cats all day. She'd even gone over to her mom and dad's, and had found her parental unit looking decidedly happy for some reason, but of their four felines there was not a single trace.

"Maybe they've gone to the park?" Chase suggested. "They go there every night."

"Yeah, but not without saying goodbye, and not before they've eaten their fill."

Max and Dooley hadn't touched their bowls, and neither had Harriet or Brutus.

No, something was wrong, she could feel it in her bones. Something was very wrong.

She turned on the television, to take her mind off her cats for a moment, and her uncle's abduction, and great was her surprise when suddenly her mom and dad's faces appeared right there on the screen!

"What the...." she said as she sat up with a jerk and turned up the volume. And both she and Chase watched with rising indignation as her mom and dad were interviewed by a reporter from WLBC-9, about some money they'd apparently won in the lottery!

"So that's why Mom and Dad were acting so weird! They saw Madame Solange and now they've gone and won the lottery!"

"But why didn't they tell us?"

"I don't know!" She swung her feet from the bed. "But I'm going to find out!"

"But, honey, they're probably asleep."

"I don't care! They lied to me!"

"They didn't exactly lie to you. They just didn't tell you what they were up to."

"Withholding information is the same thing as lying!"

"Come on, babe. Can't this wait until tomorrow?"

"No, it can't!" she said, and was thundering down the stairs before he could stop her.

Moments later she was charging into her parents' house, stomping up the stairs, and bursting into their bedroom, where they, too, were watching the same broadcast!

Judging from the sheepish looks they gave her, they knew very well they did something they shouldn't have.

"Honey, we can explain," said her mother.

"You hate those fortune tellers, and so you should!" Dad added.

"So when Madame Solange said we'd win the lottery, we decided not to tell you because—"

"—you would have been upset—"

"—and we didn't want to jinx things."

"And now we won!" said Dad. "So yay!"

"I don't believe you played the lottery," said Odelia, "while Uncle Alec is languishing in some hellhole somewhere, hoping we're working around the clock to save his life!"

"But, honey, what can we do?" asked her mom.

"Yeah, we're not cops!" said her dad.

"No, but you're family," she countered. Both her mom and dad hung their heads, and suddenly she felt sorry for them, and embarrassed by her outburst. "Look, I'm sorry, all right," she said, taking a seat at the foot of the bed. "How much did you win?"

Both heads came up again, and a gleam appeared in her parents' eyes. "Fifty thousand smackeroos!" said her dad.

"And we're going to spend it on a cruise!" her mom added.

"And your wedding, of course," said her dad.

"Oh, Dad," said Odelia with a sigh. She glanced over to the television. "So Madame Solange is the real deal, huh? Maybe she can tell us where Uncle Alec is?"

"Hey, that's a great idea!" said Mom. "We'll go tomorrow. I'm sure she'll be able to tell us where Alec is in a heartbeat." She thunked her head. "Why didn't I think of this sooner?"

Just then, Chase entered the room, looking a little trepidatious. "Um, I just got a call from Dolores," he said, holding up his phone. "Your grandmother and Scarlett have just been arrested for trespassing. They tried to break into Town Hall for some reason."

Now three members of the Poole family thunked their heads.

"Oh, and also?" the cop continued, clearly nervous to be standing in the bedroom of his future in-laws. "They claim Charlene killed Alec, so that's an interesting development."

19

*L*ook, Charlene Butterwick is a perfectly nice person, don't get me wrong, but spending the night at the foot of her bed wasn't exactly the same thing as spending the night at the foot of my own human's bed.

I'm not saying that in due course I wouldn't have grown to love and appreciate Charlene, especially since she kept feeding us morsels of the tastiest food I'd eaten in quite a while, but as of this moment I was starting to feel that Gran hadn't done us a great service by giving us away to her future daughter-in-law.

"I don't know how much longer I can take this, Max," said Harriet, clearly of the same opinion. "I mean, Charlene is a great person and all, and the food is just to die for, but honestly? I'd much rather be home right now and eating some of our regular kibble."

"Me, too," Brutus grunted. "And the first chance I get I'm staging an escape."

"Oh, can I come, too, Brutus?" asked Dooley. "I miss my usual spot on the couch."

88

20

"What were you thinking, Ma?" said Marge, not very pleased with her mother's latest stunt. They'd managed to bail both her and Scarlett out of jail, but that didn't mean they were out of the woods yet.

"I was thinking that Charlene Butterwick is blackmailing Alec, that's what I was thinking," said Gran as she rubbed her back, sore from spending the past hour in the slammer.

"You should really invest in some nicer accommodations," said Scarlett, addressing the duty sergeant who was busy drawing up the release papers. "Maybe a nice sofa, and a television. This is the twenty-first century, you know, not the middle ages."

They were still at the police station, waiting for the final hurdles to be passed before Gran and her friend were free again. "You should be glad they're releasing you now," said Odelia, like her mother very unhappy with her grandmother's shenanigans. Not least of all because she hated spending the night at the police station and not in her warm bed at home. "They could have easily kept you here until you appeared in front of the judge."

"Oh, nonsense," said Gran, waving an irritable hand. "All we did was try to make sure my son doesn't get caught in a loveless marriage with a manipulative bride. And since when is that a crime?"

"It's a crime when it involves breaking into Town Hall in the middle of the night," said Chase, not unreasonably. He'd been most instrumental in securing the two elderly ladies' early release, but so far they hadn't exactly shown him any gratitude, only a lot of lip.

"Look, it's pretty obvious that Charlene's got something on my son," said Gran now. "Or else he wouldn't rush into this marriage without bothering to tell his mother first."

Odelia shared a look with her own mother, and her dad, too. "I think we better tell her," she said now. "Before she gets into any more trouble."

"Tell me what?" said Gran. Then stomped an irritable foot. "I knew it! I knew there was something you weren't telling me! She's pregnant, isn't she? And that's why they're going ahead with this shotgun wedding!"

"Ma, you better sit down," said Odelia's mother as she led her mom to a nearby bench.

"Oh, it's that bad, huh?" said Gran, giving her daughter a worried look. "What is it? Did Alec kill someone and Charlene found out about it and now she's blackmailing him?"

"No!" said Mom, rolling her eyes. "Why do you always have to assume the worst?"

"Because I know my son, and I know he's probably got a lot of bodies buried all over the place. Buried them and threw away the keys."

"What keys? What bodies!" Mom cried.

"Ask him—*he* knows," said Gran, giving Chase a pointed look.

"Lord give me strength," said Chase, closing his eyes and rubbing his face.

"The thing is, Ma," said Mom, "that Alec was abducted. He and Charlene were home last night when suddenly three men forced their way in and took Alec."

"What?" said Gran, frowning. "What are you talking about?"

"Uncle Alec was taken, Gran," said Odelia, crouching down in front of her grandmother and taking her hands in hers. "But we're doing everything in our power to get him back, so please don't worry, all right?"

"My son? Taken?" asked Gran, looking distinctly startled. "I don't get it. What's this gotta do with this wedding thing?"

"Well, one of the demands the kidnappers made was that Charlene had to announce the wedding in the local paper," Mom explained.

"That makes no sense whatsoever," said Scarlett, who'd also taken a seat and was rubbing her calves now. "Who are these kidnappers? Huey, Dewey and Louie?"

"It is a little unorthodox," Odelia admitted.

"Unorthodox?" said Gran. "Unorthodox is when Father Reilly invites Morris dancers to liven up his service. This is just plain nuts."

"How long have you known about this?" asked Scarlett.

"Well, since it happened," said Mom, a little ruefully.

"And you didn't think to tell us?" asked Gran.

"We didn't want you to worry," said Dad. "Your heart—"

"My heart is fine—better than yours!" Gran made to get up, but Mom sat her down again.

"Now promise me you won't do anything stupid, Ma. Promise."

"I never do anything stupid," Gran growled. "It's you that does all the stupid stuff, like not telling me my son has been kidnapped by Donald Duck's nephews. Let's get out of here, Scarlett. We've got a police chief to find."

"Wait a minute," said Odelia. "Have you seen the cats? I can't seem to find them anywhere."

"I gave them to Charlene as a wedding present," said Gran, before walking out of the police station, leaving the rest of her family to stare after her.

"So much for not doing anything stupid," murmured Odelia's dad.

🐾

olf Moonblood stared out across his domain. Standing in the trailer he shared with his one true love Solange Moonblood, he'd built himself an empire: the biggest and most popular circus on the East Coast. The fact that he now saw the big top of Circus Moonblood rise above the rest of the fairground, dwarfing the many other stalls and trailers and attractions filled him with a distinct sense of pride.

He'd done all that. He'd made Circus Moonblood the success story it was today.

"Wolf?" asked a sleepy voice from the bed. "What are you doing?"

"I can't sleep," grunted the tall and imposing circus director.

"Come back to bed, sweetheart," said Solange, patting the space beside her.

Wolf gazed out at the fairground, its lights twinkling invitingly in spite of the late hour, and drained the last of his herbal tea, then stomped through the trailer he and Solange shared and sat down on the edge of the bunk.

"What's on your mind?" asked Solange, rubbing his broad back.

"Strange dreams," he grunted. "Dreams of a life I didn't even know existed."

"What kind of life?" asked Solange, a tinge of worry in her melodious voice. With her long fair hair and her striking green eyes she was a remarkable appearance.

"I can't recall," said the circus owner. "Something about... cats."

"That's not so bad, is it? Cats are important." Circus Moonblood prided itself in its collection of big cats: they had tigers, lions, and even a puma, whose roar could often be heard in the middle of the night.

Wolf nodded, and rubbed his rust-colored mustache. His rugged features and sizable bulk never failed to impress. He was a father figure to the group of entertainers the circus traveled with, but also a force to be reckoned with—a giant of a man.

"Go back to sleep," said Solange. "Did you drink the tea my sister made you?"

"I did."

"It'll help you sleep. Just lie down and soon those dreams will be a thing of the past."

"I hope so," he said, stretching himself out on the bunk. "I don't like these dreams, Solange. They make me feel... uneasy in my mind."

Solange smiled and planted a sweet kiss on his cheek. "It's this town," she said. "I've told you from the beginning there's something very strange about this town. Soon we'll move on, and those dreams will disappear."

"Good," he growled, and soon was asleep once more.

§

Solange stared down at her partner, and as soon as he'd tumbled into a restless sleep, her smile disappeared and a frown appeared on her alabaster brow. The tea was working, but still she wasn't satisfied. These dreams

Wolf kept having troubled her. She vowed to talk to her sister again tomorrow, to see if nothing further could be done.

The circus depended on Wolf's good health and untroubled state of mind, and frankly her own personal happiness depended on him, too.

She hated seeing him like this. And as she lay down next to her husband, she considered moving along before their time in Hampton Cove was up. Clearly this town was having a detrimental influence, and the sooner they left it in their rearview mirror, the better.

21

*C*harlene had slept but fitfully. She was, of course, used to dealing with stress and the pressures that came with being mayor of a small town, but she'd never been the victim of a home invasion before, and she didn't really think she was handling things very well.

And as she opened her eyes, she became aware of four cats' eyes staring at her intently from the foot of the bed, and groaned.

Just what she needed right now: the added responsibility of four pets.

At least two of them she could hand back to their owners, but the others? How had she ever allowed herself to be convinced it was a good idea to suddenly adopt two cats?

And as she rubbed the sleep from her eyes, the plaintive meows of the biggest cat of the bunch made itself heard. It was a sound that cut through her like a knife, and was not to be ignored.

So maybe this was a good thing? At least now she'd have to get out of bed and deal with her newly acquired pets' bathroom needs.

The second cat added its voice to the choir, and soon all four cats were meowing and creating quite the spectacle. A private concert, in her own bedroom!

"All right, all right," she said, and threw off the comforter and got up. "Let's get you outside first, before you do your business all over my carpets."

The cats looked at her as if she'd just personally insulted them, and she now wished she was just like Odelia Poole and her mom and grandma: they could talk to these strange creatures, and probably understand everything they said.

She slipped her feet into her slippers and tied the sash of her dressing gown around her and then slouched out of the room, her hair a mess, and her eyes puffy.

She didn't care. If her neighbors wanted to snap pictures of her and post them on their Instagram or Facebook, they could go right ahead and do it.

She noticed how two of the cats didn't have collars, so she took a couple of dog collars from her closet, part of a shipment destined for the animal shelter, and tied them to the cats' necks. If they weren't totally at ease with the procedure, she decided to ignore them. She couldn't risk them running off. The Pooles would kill her if they did.

And so it was that ten minutes later Charlene Butterwick, Mayor of Hampton Cove, could be seen wandering around the neighborhood, walking four cats, who were plaintively meowing all the while, looking like something the cats dragged in—or out.

"*L*ook," said Mom, pointing in the direction of a pink-clad figure on the sidewalk. "It's Charlene. Oh, and she's walking our cats!"

Odelia stared at the lonely figure. "She looks terrible," she said, and that was an understatement. Charlene's hair was a mess, and she was wearing a pink housecoat that had seen better days, her feet stuck in a pair of old slippers, her eyes half closed.

The cats, meanwhile, looked distinctly unhappy and were tugging at their leashes.

"I don't think she's a cat person," said Mom with a shake of the head.

"No, definitely not," Odelia agreed.

She quickly parked the car and both women got out. They'd waited until now to go and fetch their cats, even though Odelia had wanted to drop by Charlene's house the moment she'd learned Gran had 'given away' their cats to the Mayor. But Mom had convinced her that showing up on the woman's doorstep in the middle of the night was a bad idea, so she'd decided to wait until morning.

At the crack of dawn she'd gotten up, met her mom in front of the house, and they'd set off on their cat rescue mission.

"I can't believe Gran would give away our cats," said Odelia for the umpteenth time.

"Yeah, of all the stunts she's ever pulled this one takes the cake," said Mom. "Charlene! Hi!" she said, waving at the Mayor.

"Oh, hiya, Marge," said Charlene. "Odelia. Any news?" she asked eagerly.

"Nothing yet," said Odelia. "But we're working on it." Or rather Chase was working on it. "Um, so I see you've got our cats there?"

Charlene glanced down, as if seeing the cats for the first time. "Oh, that's right. Vesta dropped them off yesterday. She said they were a wedding gift, and the other two I found wandering in the street last night so I took them in."

"The thing is, Charlene," said Mom, "that my mother has an eccentric streak."

"What she means is that Gran didn't ask our permission to give away the cats," Odelia specified.

"Oh," said Charlene, and frowned as she processed this.

"Are you all right, honey?" asked Mom, her voice laced with concern. "You don't look so hot."

"Yeah, I don't know what's wrong with me," said Charlene, shaking her head as if trying to clear it. "I've been feeling really weird ever since Alec was taken. Not myself, if you know what I mean. Foggy in my mind."

"Yeah, I can see you're not yourself," said Odelia. "Do you want us to take you to see my dad?"

"Your dad?" asked Charlene vaguely, her eyes glazing over and swaying like a reed in the breeze.

"We better put you in the car," said Mom, and supported the Mayor before she toppled over. "Take her other arm, honey. That's it. Nice and easy. There we go."

And together both women escorted Charlene into Odelia's pickup. The moment they had, the woman simply keeled over on the backseat and became unresponsive.

"Oh, dear," said Mom. "I think she lost consciousness, honey."

"Let's take her to see Dad," said Odelia, then gestured for her cats to jump into the car, and they didn't hesitate one moment but all eagerly did as she suggested.

"Shouldn't we lock up Charlene's house or something?" asked Mom, darting a quick look at the Mayor's residence.

"She locked it before she set out for our morning walk," said Max.

"Yeah, she locked it up tight," said Harriet, sounding distinctly unhappy.

A fly had managed to sneak into the car, and Odelia swatted at it now, before Max said, "Please don't kill my friend. That's Norm," he explained to the stunned women. "Norm has been helping us find Uncle Alec."

And as Odelia started the engine, she shared a look of concern with her mother. Talking cats was one thing, but a fly? Life was quickly becoming very interesting indeed.

22

I was so happy to see my human again I would have jumped into her arms if she hadn't been trying to steer her car through morning traffic.

"We thought we'd never escape," I said eagerly.

"Yeah, Charlene is a nice person and all," said Harriet, "but that house of hers is like a fortress. No way in or out!"

"She does have some nice meat to offer," said Brutus, stressing one of the Mayor's many positive points.

"She's no Odelia, though," said Dooley, pointing out the main negative aspect of the matter.

Odelia shot us a look of concern through the rearview mirror. "If I'd known Gran was going to give you away I would have stopped her. You know that, right?"

"Problem is that my mother never announces her crazy ideas before she sets them in motion," Marge explained in an apologetic tone. "So I'm truly sorry you guys had to go through this, and I wish I could promise you it will never happen again, but I'm afraid I can't."

"But we are going to have a long talk with Gran and explain to her that our cats are not chattel. You're part of the family, and you simply don't give away family members as if they were a mere toy or gadget."

Odelia sounded upset, and so did Marge, and I shouldn't wonder. I did have one minor point to add to the conversation, though. "I don't think she actually meant to give us away for good, though," I said. "It's entirely possible this was just a ruse on her part to smuggle us into Charlene's house, along with the rest of the bugs."

"Bugs? What bugs?" asked Marge, turning to face me. She was riding shotgun while her daughter gunned the engine and practically flew along the road.

"Gran planted a lot of bugs in Charlene's house," Dooley explained. "And she said she was going to plant more bugs in Charlene's car and in her office, too." He paused. "I asked if these bugs were dangerous but Gran said they weren't."

"But why?" asked Marge. "Why bug Charlene's home and office?"

"And her car," said Dooley. "Don't forget about the car."

Marge smiled as she patted my friend on the head. "I'm not forgetting, honey."

"The thing is that Gran thinks that Charlene is somehow blackmailing Uncle Alec into marrying her," I explained. "Which is why she felt the need to smuggle Dooley and myself into the house, and plant all of those bugs."

Marge turned to face the front again, a set look on her face. "Can I kill her, Odelia?"

"If you want to risk life in prison," said Odelia.

"Oh, I'm starting to think it's worth it."

For a moment, we rode on in silence, and then Norm said, "I think this is so cool, the way you guys can talk to your humans. I wish I could talk to my human." He paused, then added, "If I had a human, that is."

"Don't flies have an owner?" asked Dooley, interested.

"No, I'm afraid we don't," said Norm. "We're free as the

proverbial bird."

"Who are you talking to, Dooley?" asked Odelia.

"Norm," said Dooley. "He's a fly who's as free as a bird."

"Crazy," Odelia muttered. "Absolutely nuts."

"Oh, that's right," I said. "Norm told us about the lottery win, Marge. So how much did you win?"

"Um, fifty thousand," said Marge, darting a quick look at her daughter, whose face had taken on the same set look her mom had displayed before.

Harriet cleared her throat. "I have a little bit of news to share, too," she said.

"Go ahead, honey," said Marge. "What is it?"

"Well, Brutus and I took a witness statement last night from a witness who witnessed the kidnapping of Uncle Alec, and this witness witnessed three men taking Uncle Alec out of Charlene's house. Our witness also had a very good description to offer."

And she proceeded to fill Marge and Odelia in on all the details pertaining to the case. She didn't mention that her witness was a dog, but then that was probably a given.

Odelia was tickled pink by this development, and promised to tell her boyfriend straight away. Harriet looked extremely happy, and gave me a look that spoke volumes. "So you see, Max, Brutus and I are really coming into our own as detectives," she said, rubbing it in as much as she could.

"I know," I said, not begrudging her this success.

"Pretty soon we'll be Hampton Cove's premier feline sleuths," she continued with an airy glance out the window.

"That's great," I said.

"Overtaking you and Dooley," she added.

"This is not a competition, sweetie," said Marge from the front seat. "Though you did really good there, I must say. You and Brutus both."

"For your information, Marge," said Harriet decidedly,

"life *is* a competition."

"No, it's not," said Marge. "Cooperation is what we need to find my brother, and I hope you don't forget that."

Harriet gave her human a look of confusion. "You mean…"

"I mean that the best results are often achieved when we all work together, not try to best one another. So try to work as a team, Harriet, that's all I'm saying."

"Oh," said Harriet, taken aback by this strange advice. "Work as a team?"

"Yep. Cooperation, not competition, that's the secret of success. Park right there, honey," she told her daughter, and soon Odelia had parked behind a very large SUV and we were getting out. Charlene, who'd been dozing, was gently awakened by Odelia, and assisted out of the car and across the street, then marched into Tex's doctor's office.

"Teamwork," said Harriet, still ruminating on Marge's words as we all waited patiently on the sidewalk for our humans' return. "Cooperation, not competition," she murmured, as if the concept was completely alien to her. Then she glanced up at me. "Do you think Marge was joking, Max?"

"No, I think she was absolutely serious when she said that," I intimated. "We're much better when we all work together as a team, Harriet. And you know that."

"Huh," she said, then shrugged. "Okay, fine. So let's join forces from now on, shall we? You and Dooley go this way, and Brutus and I will go that way. And may the best team win." And with these words, she was off in the direction of Hampton Cove's Main Street.

Dooley and I stared after her, and then Dooley said, "I don't think Harriet has entirely grasped the meaning of the word teamwork yet, Max."

"No," I said. "I don't think she has."

"Whatcha doing, Chief?"

Chase looked up from his computer to see that Dolores Peltz, the police station dispatcher, was standing next to his desk. She was holding a steaming mug of coffee in her hands that said, 'World's Greatest Cop,' and was taking occasional sips.

"Oh, just looking at mug shots," he said, and gestured to his screen, where a gallery of the world's skeeviest-looking criminals was on display.

"Who ya looking for?" asked Dolores, narrowing her eyes at the screen.

"All I've got is a description," said Chase, and read from his notebook, "Heavy build, crooked nose, shaven head, cauliflower ears, Boston accent. Oh, and drives an old dark-green Ford van."

"I'd start with the van," said Dolores. "What case is this?"

"Um…" He couldn't very well tell her it was actually the case of their missing Chief, so he said, "Burglary. On Grover Street."

"Burglary? I don't know anything about no burglary. Who's the victim?"

"Um..." He closed his computer. "You know, Dolores, I was going through the calendar and I saw that your birthday is coming up soon."

Dolores grimaced. "Don't remind me. Once you get to be my age any birthday is a birthday too much. Why, are you and the guys cooking me up a surprise?"

"Aren't we always? I was just wondering if there's something special you would like."

"Oh, there's plenty," said the dispatcher. "Where do I start?"

"Maybe make a list? And then we can get you something you really want, instead of some corny gift you don't need."

"Like last year, you mean. I could have done without that balloon ride, buddy. You know I hate heights."

"I know now," Chase said. When Dolores had discovered she'd been gifted a free ride in a balloon, she'd screamed the entire precinct down, until they'd agreed to exchange the gift for a day at the spa instead.

And as Chase watched Dolores stalk off, he breathed a sigh of relief. If Dolores found out what was going on, so would the rest of town. And he didn't want to endanger his superior officer's life by blabbing about his kidnapping.

Suddenly a cry rang out through the police station main office, and Chase quickly walked out of his own office to see what was going on. When he got there, he saw that all of his officers stood gathered around Officer Sarah Flunk, who was... crying!

"What's going on?" he asked, joining the throng. "Sarah? Are you all right?"

"Better than all right, boss," said the copper-haired officer, wiping her freckled face. "I'm getting married!"

"Oh," he said, not expecting this. "And you're not happy about it, is that it?"

"I'm very happy! Very, very happy!" said the young officer. "I never thought Barry would propose. I kept hoping, and wishing, and now, all of a sudden, he sent me a text. Here." And she pressed her phone into his hands. On the screen the message read, 'I know I should have done this a lot sooner, but… will you please marry me? Barry.'

"It couldn't be happening to a nicer person," Dolores grunted.

"I'm going to marry Barry!" Sarah squealed, and drew cheers from her colleagues.

Chase smiled, and joined the others in congratulating his young colleague.

Which is why he was so surprised when he returned to his own office and found Barry Billong sitting in front of his desk, looking distinctly unhappy.

"Barry, I believe congratulations are in order!" said Chase, and extended his hand to the moon-faced young man, who took it limply, and shook it without much enthusiasm.

"Please close the door, Detective Kingsley," said Barry, darting nervous glances at the door.

Chase, wondering what was going on, closed the door and took a seat behind his desk.

"I managed to slip in unseen," said Barry, now chewing his fingernails and looking like a man hunted by a posse of bounty hunters. "But I'm not sure I'll be able to get out without being noticed. And that's okay. But first I wanted to talk to you, sir."

"Okay," said Chase, smiling at the guy. "What's going on, Barry? Why aren't you happy? You're getting married to a lovely girl."

"That's just it," said Barry, leaning forward and swallowing nervously, his Adam's apple bobbing up and down like a jack-in-the-box. "I don't want to get married to Sarah. You see, I'm engaged to be married to... another girl. You don't know her, but I already met her parents and everything. So now I'm engaged to two girls, and it's simply too much."

Chase would have agreed that being engaged to two girls was probably one too many, but since he liked and respected Sarah Flunk tremendously, the overwhelming emotion he now felt was one of anger. "You've been two-timing Sarah all this time? Stringing her along? Is that what you're telling me?"

"Don't look at me like that, Detective," said Barry in a whiny voice, holding up his hands in a gesture of defense. "I fell in love with Francine around the same time I met Sarah, and one thing led to another and... I never thought things with Sarah would actually develop into... whatever it is we have. But every time I tried to break up with her, she seemed so heartbroken, and so I could never actually go through with it. I tried to, but..." He hung his head. "I guess I'm just a coward."

"But if you didn't want to get married to Sarah, why did you propose to her?"

"That's just it—I never wanted to propose. It's just that these two guys... They said if I didn't send that message they'd break my legs, and I like my legs, Detective. I like them the way they are. So they watched as I typed, and even gave me suggestions as to the exact wording of the message. They were very... insistent."

Chase frowned. "What guys? What are you talking about?"

"I don't know who they are. I never met them before! They showed up at the dealership this morning and asked if they could take the new Toyota Yaris for a spin, and so they did, and then they parked along the road and said that if I

111

didn't propose to Sarah right there and then they'd break my legs, and then they'd break my arms, and maybe my neck, too —they hadn't decided."

"Can you describe these men?" asked Chase, thinking this was one hell of a story Barry was telling him.

"Well, they were very big, both of them, and very hairy, too, and one of them had a tattoo of a skull and crossbones on the side of his neck. Um… Oh, yeah, and they said that if I told anyone about this they'd break my legs, and my arms, and maybe my neck, too." He sighed. "I had the impression they'd done this sort of thing before."

"Organized crime?" Chase suggested.

Barry nodded. "It was a very stressful experience, Detective, and they didn't even buy the Yaris, so I've got nothing to show for my trouble, which caused my boss to yell at me."

"I think you better come clean to Sarah, Barry," said Chase. "You can't keep stringing her along, and now you've gone and made things worse with this bogus proposal."

"But if I tell her they'll break my legs and my arms… and my neck!"

"They'll never know, Barry. Just tell Sarah the whole story, and leave nothing out." He leaned forward. "Because if you don't? I'll be the one breaking your legs, and your arms, and your neck—is that understood?"

The car salesman inadvertently touched his neck and nodded furiously, then got up.

The moment the guy had left his office, Chase thought for a moment, gazing out the window of his office at the parking lot right outside the station, and then at Town Hall beyond it. Strange things were happening in this town of his, and he wasn't sure what to make of it. He certainly wished the Chief was there to help him figure it out, though.

24

$\mathcal{T}$ex looked up in surprise when his wife and daughter entered the room, a dazed-looking Charlene Butterwick supported between them.

"You better take a look at her, honey," said Marge. "I think something is very wrong."

"She collapsed in the middle of the street just now," Odelia added.

Immediately he instructed the Mayor to be laid down on his consultation table and as he shone a light into her eyes, he immediately saw that Marge was right: Charlene's pupil response was not what it should be.

"It looks like she's been drugged," he said after a moment. "Charlene? Charlene, honey, did you take any pills in the last twenty-four hours? Sleeping pills maybe?"

But Charlene shook her head. "I hate sleeping pills," she said sleepily, slurring her words a little. "They make me feel so... sssleepy."

"I think we should take her to the hospital," said Tex. "Do a blood test to find out what she's taken. She's clearly under the influence of something, that much I can tell you."

"Do you think the same people who took Uncle Alec gave her something?" asked Odelia. "Maybe injected her with something?"

"Could be," said Tex, as he sat Charlene upright again and did a few more tests to ascertain if the Mayor needed an ambulance or if she would be able to make it to the hospital under her own steam. "Her vital signs are good," he murmured after checking her pulse and having a listen to her heart. "I don't think she's in any immediate danger. But I'd like to have her admitted just in case."

"We'll take her," said Odelia. "Charlene? Can you walk?" she asked, and the Mayor nodded.

"Oh, sure," she said. "I'm a big walker. You should see me walking. I'm great at walking." And as she got up off the table, she immediately went down and fell flat on the floor.

❧

*W*hen they got out of her dad's doctor's office, Odelia noticed to her dismay that her cats had all skedaddled. At least this time they probably hadn't been kidnapped and given away as a wedding present—she hoped!

They drove Charlene to the hospital, where they promised them they'd take really good care of her, and then Odelia dropped her mom off at the library so she could finally start her working day, before heading into the office herself.

Dan Goory, when she arrived, was waiting for her, looking distinctly concerned.

"You didn't have to come in, honey," he said when he saw her. "I would have understood. What with your uncle having gone missing and all."

Dan was the only person outside of the family Odelia had confided in, knowing he wouldn't blab about it.

"No, it's fine," she said. "I better keep working. Otherwise I just keep running through the whole sequence of events in my mind over and over again, and there's nothing I can do anyway."

"Is Chase making any progress?" asked her boss, caressing his long white beard, a look of concern in his lively eyes.

"There have been some developments," she said, "but nothing concrete, I'm afraid."

Dan nodded. "I don't know what this town is coming to, when the chief of police himself gets kidnapped. Maybe you should arrange for some extra security for your family?"

"I'm sure that Chase will protect us," she said, taking a seat behind her desk.

"I saw your mom and dad on TV last night," said her editor, a smile making his beard waggle. "Did they really win the lottery?"

"Yeah, they did," she said, also smiling a tired smile now. "Though they didn't exactly win it fair and square," she added, her frown returning. And she told the Gazette editor about what happened.

"So the winning ticket arrived in the mail? That's odd."

"Yeah, clearly someone wanted them to win."

"But who?"

She shrugged. "A well-wisher? One of Dad's patients, expressing their gratitude?"

"Something peculiar happened to me, too," said Dan as he took a seat on the edge of her desk. "You know how I've always wanted to complete my train set, right? The one I started years ago?"

Odelia remembered he'd built an elaborate train set in his attic. He'd once shown it to her, and it was pretty amazing. It took up half the space, and consisted of an entire town built around the train set now, complete with hills, bridges, tunnels and small houses and cars and people. He'd spent the best part of a decade building it.

"Well, the key part of my collection had been missing until now: the D-4560 locomotive."

"Only three remaining models exist," she said, nodding. He'd told her the story many times, how he'd tried to buy it but failed, since the price of the coveted model locomotive was upwards of a hundred grand now.

"Last night I got a delivery," said the aged newspaper chief, his face splitting into a smile, "and lo and behold, it contained the D-4560! And in pristine condition, too!"

"But... how is that possible?"

"I don't know, but it looks like some secret admirer must have sent it to me."

"No address on the package?"

"None. But I'm not looking a gift horse in the mouth, Odelia. I'm keeping it and sending my silent thanks to whoever shipped it to me."

"Well, that's great," she said. He looked as happy as a kid on Christmas morning, and she thought it couldn't have happened to a nicer person.

"And the strange thing is," said Dan as he got up, "that that woman predicted this would happen, and then it did!"

"What woman?"

"Well, Madame Solange, of course. Didn't I tell you I went to see her a couple of days ago? I told her about this hobby of mine, and she said I was going to come into possession of the locomotive very soon now. I didn't believe her at the time, of course," he said, patting the doorjamb as he walked out. "But now I definitely do!"

Odelia stared after her boss as he turned into his own office, whistling a merry tune as he did, and blinked. Madame Solange. First she predicted Mom and Dad's lottery win, and now Dan's locomotive. Maybe it was time she paid a visit to this mysterious fortune teller, and asked her if she knew where Uncle Alec was. She wasn't a big believer in that sort of thing, but frankly she was willing to try anything to get her beloved uncle back.

25

"𝓘 like this espionage business, Max," said Norm as he buzzed along over our heads. "I think maybe I missed my calling in life. I should have been a spy."

"That's great, Norm," I said as we pranced along the sidewalk in search of a potential witness who could tell us what had happened to Odelia's uncle.

"So is it true that flies feed on the kind of stuff that us cats think is a little gross?" asked Dooley.

"What do you mean, gross?" asked Norm.

"Well, things like garbage, and, um, horse manure?"

"And pig shit," I said. "And cow dung."

"Oh, sure. I love me a good helping of cow dung," said Norm, showing no shame at his choice of nourishment whatsoever, and nor he should, as far as I was concerned. "Though what I like most, of course, is a good, thick pile of elephant dung."

"Elephant dung?" I asked with a laugh. "Where do you find elephants around here?" And then I remembered the parade from the day before. "Oh, you mean the fairground?"

"Sure. I've been spending a lot of time over there, and the food they've got at that place is simply to die for. Yum-my!"

"Better you than me, Norm," I said, the thought of elephant dung not exactly filling me with relish.

We'd arrived at the General Store, where one of our main sources of information was lazily lounging on his owner's checkout counter, not a care in the world.

Wilbur Vickery, meanwhile, sat ringing up the wares his customers were dumping on the conveyor belt. He was looking pretty chipper, I thought.

Kingman opened a lazy eye when we approached and then closed it again. "Come back later, fellas," he said. "I'm just having the best dream of my life and you're ruining it." Then, moments later, he opened his eyes again with a sigh. "Yeah, it's gone. What do you want? And can you please get rid of this horrible fly?"

"Oh, this is Norm, Kingman," said Dooley. "He's our friend."

Kingman gave Dooley a critical look. "I think I must have misheard you, buddy. For a moment there I thought you said you're friends with a fly. But that's impossible, because as we all know flies are the harbingers of death and decay. They feed on crap and then carry that same crap onto our shiny coats of fur, which is a very rude thing to do indeed."

"I promise I'll never carry any dung onto your fur, good sir," said Norm now.

"And it speaks," said Kingman with a sigh. "Of course it does."

"Our human has gone missing, Kingman," I said, deciding to cut right to the chase and develop the theme I'd come to discuss. "Uncle Alec? He was taken from the home of his girl-friend two nights ago and hasn't been seen since."

"I thought he was getting married? Wasn't there some-thing in the paper yesterday? It's gotten a big buzz all around town. Even Wilbur couldn't shut up about it. I think he's got a thing for the Mayor himself, so the announcement hit him pretty hard."

"Yeah, that announcement was bogus," I said. "One of the demands the kidnappers made was to print it in the Gazette. We have no idea why."

"The weirdest thing," Kingman agreed. "But then things have gotten a little weird around here lately. Did you know that Wilbur received a wedding proposal from an English princess? Girl named Frances. She's supposed to be Prince Charles's third child, though as far as I'm aware Prince Charles only has two kids, both boys. But this Princess Frances wrote a long letter, saying how she saw Wilbur's picture on his Facebook page and immediately fell head over heels in love with him and now she wants to marry him."

We glanced up at Wilbur, whose stubbled jaw was working furiously as he watched a Droopy cartoon on the small television he keeps next to his cash register, and abruptly burst into raucous laughter, spitting out a piece of beef jerky he'd been chewing on.

"Why anyone would want to marry that guy is beyond me," said Norm, and I think he spoke for all of us.

"An English princess?" I said, figuring I hadn't heard right.

"Yah," said Kingman.

"The only daughter of the future king of England."

"Yah."

"Has fallen head over heels in love with Wilbur?"

"Yah. Pretty damn weird, huh? And even weirder? Just before this letter arrived, carrying the official letterhead of Buckingham Palace and everything, Wilbur had gone to see this psychic at the fair? And she'd told him he would meet a genuine blue blood soon and would marry into one of the most famous royal families in the world. So now Wilbur figures it was all meant to be." The spreading cat sighed and placed his head on his paws. "I just hope I'll get along with these Corgis. I hear they're pretty tough little buggers."

I'd met the Queen's corgis, and I could confirm that they were, indeed, pretty tough, but since I didn't think Wilbur stood a snowball's chance in hell of getting hitched with the non-existent daughter of Prince Charles, I didn't even want to waste my breath telling him about this. Instead, I said, "So no news on Uncle Alec, I presume?"

"Nope. Haven't seen the guy, and haven't heard anything about this mysterious disappearance either, I'm afraid." He glanced at Norm, who'd taken a seat on a loaf of bread placed behind the counter. "Don't you dare, Norm," he said warningly.

"Oh, hold your horses, big cat," said Norm, taking flight again. "I wasn't going to relieve myself if that's what you're thinking."

"I know what you flies are like," grunted Kingman.

"Well, I happen to be a clean fly," said Norm. "And so I don't simply relieve myself on any old object I come across."

"Good for you," said Kingman, and closed his eyes again, indicating our audience was at an end.

So we took our leave, and as we walked along, Dooley said, "Do you really think Wilbur will be moving to England soon, Max? And maybe become the next king?"

"No, I don't, Dooley," I said. "I think someone is playing a cruel trick on Wilbur, and I'd very much like to find out who is behind this letter from this so-called Princess Frances."

"It's true, you know," said Norm. "I pick the places I do my business in or on very carefully. I have strict rules about that—rules I learned dandling on my mother's knee."

"Do flies dandle on their mother's knee?" I asked, surprised.

"Oh, sure. And she never failed to tell me that the best way to earn the respect of my peers is to do my business where no one will notice. Like on black toilet seats. Or in people's stews, or in a baker's freshly prepared dough. Or on the hood of dark sedans. Or even in a cup of coffee. People never notice when I take a tiny dump in their cup of coffee, and I like to think it adds that little bit of extra flavor a nice cup of coffee needs."

I swallowed away a lump of uneasiness. Somehow I had a feeling that our newly formed friendship with Norm the fly was akin to dancing with the devil. Or worse!

26

*V*esta Muffin and Scarlett Canyon were seated in the outdoor dining area of the Hampton Cove Star again, their usual haunt when they weren't trying to break into Town Hall, or planting bugs in mayoral homes.

"I think Charlene did it," said Vesta now as she took a sip from her hot chocolate, a layer of foamy cream taking residence on her upper lip.

Scarlett stared at the phenomenon, then said, "Have you thought about shaving off that mustache of yours? If you want I can do it for you."

"What mustache? I don't have a mustache."

"Yeah, you do. I would have a mustache, if I didn't kill the sucker every week or so."

"I don't know what you're talking about," Vesta grumbled as she licked the foam from her upper lip and inadvertently touched a finger to the spot under discussion.

"Waxing is best, of course," said Scarlett, taking a sip from her own flat white, to which she'd added a small helping of liquor from a flask she kept in her purse. After the events of last night she needed a pick-me-up. "Though you could try shaving, of course."

"Let's not get distracted here," said Vesta. "Did you hear what I just said or not?"

"Yeah, now you're peddling the theory that Charlene kidnapped your son. But why in heaven's name would she do that?"

"Because she's that kind of woman! Some women are nurturers, and others are kidnappers, and Charlene clearly belongs in the latter category. I think she wants my son to marry her, and Alec, who's no fool, said no way in hell, and so she's got him locked up in her basement until he cracks and in the meantime she printed the announcement in the papers to add pressure."

Scarlett cocked a skeptical eyebrow at her friend. "You think Charlene is keeping your son locked up in her basement."

"I'm sure of it."

"Like a serial killer."

"Absolutely. She's got that look in her eye."

"I think *you've* got that look in your eye, honey. The look that says you're going bananas. And I'm blaming it on that mustache. Those hairs have probably penetrated your brain and are doing some serious damage up there."

"What are you talking about?"

"Yank those suckers out, Vesta, before they make you go completely cuckoo! It's a proven fact that ingrown hair is making people lose their minds. Dementia? Alzheimer's? It's all because of those nasty little hairs. So if you just let me," she said, and leaned forward with a pair of tweezers in her hand.

"Where did those come from?" asked Vesta, recoiling.

"Let me just yank one of those suckers out and tell me how it feels."

"Don't come near me with that thing!"

"Just one, and if you don't feel an immediate relief on the brain my name isn't Scarlett Marie Gracie Canyon."

"If you touch me I'm going to smack you in the face, Scarlett—I mean it."

"You wouldn't."

"Yeah, I would."

Scarlett retracted the tweezers and tucked them into her purse. "Suit yourself. But if your brain suddenly starts going soft don't come crying to me."

"I won't. Now are you with me on this or what?"

"With you on what?"

"That's what I just said." Vesta stared at her chocolate and then took a sniff. "Did you add that filthy liquor of yours to my hot cocoa?"

"Sure," said Scarlett, slurring her words a little. "I figured you needed it, and so do I."

"You're trying to get me drunk!"

"I'm not!"

"You're the worst friend in the world, Scarlett, you know that?"

"I am not. Would the worst friend in the world try to save you from dementia, Alzheimer's and that nasty mustache?"

"Good God," said Vesta, shaking her head.

"Close, but no cigar," said Scarlett, and drained the rest of her coffee, then smacked her lips. "You know what? I think I'll have another."

Just then a camera crew suddenly materialized in front of them, and both women stared at the cameraman and the reporter who was holding his microphone aloft. The guy was wearing the most ridiculous glasses, and the most ridiculous goatee. "Do you ladies know by any chance where we can find Wilbur Vickery?" he asked chipperly.

"Over there," said Vesta automatically, pointing in the

direction of the General Store located right across the street.

"Thanks," said the guy, flashed her a toothpaste smile, and started in the direction indicated.

"Hey, aren't you going to tell us what's going on?" asked Scarlett, liquor always making her a little belligerent.

"Tune into WLBC-9, darling," said the reporter.

"Or check our website," said the camera guy with a bored expression on his face as he trudged along behind the reporter.

So Scarlett and Vesta both got out their phones and checked the local TV station's website, and sure enough Wilbur Vickery was the lead article.

They both stared at their phones for a moment, then Vesta read, in a thick voice, "Hot-blooded local shopkeeper to marry blue-blooded English rose—Madame Solange strikes it out of the park again." She glanced up at her friend. "What the hell?"

"I think it's time we go and see this Madame Solange," said Scarlett. "I want to marry a hot-blooded blue blood, too, dammit!"

"And you will, Scarlett, honey," said Vesta, patting her friend gingerly on the arm, then accidentally missing her approach shot and almost falling out of her chair. "But first we need to save my son," she added, wagging a finger in Scarlett's face and almost poking her eye out. "It's important to me. I'm all that poor boy's got, you know."

"Okay, I'll do it," said Scarlett, "but only if you let me yank out that big sucker right under your nose!" And she got out those damn tweezers again!

When the waiter in charge of the Star's outside dining area came to see if his customers were satisfied, he found Scarlett chasing her friend around, armed with some kind of weapon, and screaming, "It's for your own good, Vesta! Let me save your life!"

"*A*re you sure this is the right place?" asked Odelia as she watched a couple of kids come skipping out of a trailer, giggling all the while.

"Yes, honey. Trust me," said her mom. "Now let's do this."

It had been Odelia's idea to visit this Madame Solange and enlist her in the quest to find her uncle and Mom's brother. She hadn't told Chase, as the cop would probably think that enlisting psychics or whatever Madame Solange was, probably was taking things too far. But at this point Odelia felt that any help would be appreciated, as neither her cats nor Chase had been able to locate the missing police chief so far.

"Okay, let's just get it over with," she said and set foot for the trailer.

A burly male suddenly materialized in the doorway and gave them a look that wasn't exactly inducive to repeat customership.

"We would like to see Madame Solange," said Odelia primly. "We can pay her," she added, indicating her purse.

"Step inside," said the man. "Madame Solange will see you now."

"Thanks," said Odelia, and negotiated the three steps that led into the trailer. It was one of those brightly colored contraptions, made out of wood, painted a cheerful green, yellow and blue, and once inside she discovered it was a lot roomier than she'd expected. "This looks nice," she said. "I wonder who Madame Solange's interior decorator is."

There was a modest little waiting area, where a few chairs had been placed, and a curtained-off area where she assumed the fortune teller conducted her business.

"Um, I guess we're supposed to wait here," she said, and took a seat.

"Oh, darn," said her mom. "I forgot to bring cash. I hope she takes Visa."

"I'm sure it'll be fine," said Odelia, glancing around. All along the wall testimonials had been framed, and she read a couple of them. 'Madame Solange predicted I'd become a millionaire before my nineteenth birthday, and I did!' one read. 'Madame Solange said I'd marry my childhood sweetheart, and guess what? I'm getting married next month!' another excited testimonial read. "This Madame Solange sure has a high success rate," she said as she read a few more messages.

"Do you think she'll take a check?" Mom murmured as she rummaged around in her purse. "Looks like I forgot to bring my credit cards, too."

Odelia placed a hand on her mom's arm. "Relax, Mom. You were here before, weren't you? So you know the drill."

"Yeah, but your dad took care of everything. We should have asked him to come along."

"It'll be fine," Odelia repeated, though she was feeling a little nervous herself. She'd never been to one of these fortune tellers before, and didn't know what to expect. "So does she work with cards or a crystal ball or what?" she asked.

"Crystal ball," said Mom with a nod. "Though she hardly even looked at the thing."

Just then, the curtain was shoved aside, and Madame Solange appeared. She was younger than Odelia had expected, and prettier. Somehow she'd thought a fortune teller should be an old crone, with a hook nose, a big fat wart, and looking like an evil witch.

"Come in," said Madame Solange, giving both women a warm smile, and so Odelia took a deep breath and walked into the inner sanctum of the teller of all fortunes.

They took a seat at a small round table, and Madame Solange adjusted her robe, which was a nice brocade with gold thread, and must have cost her a pretty penny.

All around, the walls were papered with an expensive velvet wallpaper with the same gold thread, and on the floor a thick carpet lay. Subdued lighting lent the small room an intimate atmosphere, and the lack of windows made Odelia feel slightly claustrophobic, which was probably intentional. They'd clearly entered a completely different world.

"Now what can I do for you?" asked Solange, still that faint smile playing about her lips. "Oh, and before we begin, I have to warn you that this session is being filmed." She gestured to a camera that was mounted against the wall behind her, and which Odelia only now saw. "I'm being followed for a whole year," Solange explained, "as part of a documentary. They're doing a six-part series on me and the fairground in general—but me in particular," she said with a touch of pride. "So I hope you have no objections?"

"No, that's fine," said Odelia, who didn't care. "My uncle has gone missing," she said. "And I was wondering—my mom and I were wondering if you could help us find him."

"Your uncle..." said Solange, nodding, and revealed a neat

crystal ball by pulling away an intricately stitched doily. She touched the ball with her hands and closed her eyes. "Name?"

"Alec Lip," said Odelia. "He's our chief of police, and he went missing two nights ago."

"Kidnapped," said Mom, glancing intently at Solange and drinking in the woman's every move.

"Yeah, three men took him," Odelia explained, "from the home of his girlfriend, Hampton Cove's mayor Charlene Butterwick."

Solange nodded imperceptibly, her eyes still closed, then murmured, "I see him... large man, imposing... humble and well-liked in the local community..."

"Yeah, my uncle is pretty popu—"

"He's gone," said Solange abruptly, opening her eyes and adopting a more prosaic tone as she covered up her crystal ball again.

"Gone?" asked Odelia, surprised by this sudden change of demeanor. "What do you mean, gone?"

"Just that. He's gone. And he doesn't want to be found. Your uncle," said Solange with a sigh, "wasn't happy with the life he lived, so he decided he needed a break and took off."

"Took off?" asked Mom, alarmed. "Where to?"

"I can't tell you," said Solange. "Your brother doesn't want me to."

"But... you know where he is?" asked Odelia.

"Oh, sure. Madame Solange knows all. But I have to respect your uncle's wishes, so I can't tell you where he is. That'll be fifty bucks," she added, holding out her hand.

The moment they were ushered out of Madame Solange's camper, Odelia shared a look of shock with her mother. "He took off?" she said.

"I don't believe this," said Mom.

"Something's not right," said Odelia. "Obviously Solange

doesn't have a clue what happened to Uncle Alec and she's inventing some crazy story about him taking off."

"But she was right about the lottery," Mom pointed out.

Odelia was shaking her head, directing annoyed glances at the van where Solange now sat counting her money. That big burly guy was back, standing in the entrance and pointedly ignoring them. He was some kind of security person, she reckoned, making sure Madame Solange's unhappy customers couldn't lodge a complaint with the fortune teller, or demand their money back.

Just then, Odelia thought she saw a familiar figure. It was a man, built like her uncle, only this particular person had a full head of hair and a thick, red mustache. "Look at that guy over there, Mom," she said.

"Hey, he looks just like Alec," said Mom. "Only with more hair. A lot more hair."

He was dressed differently, too, with black leather pants, black leather vest, and cowboy boots. His hair was also black and slicked back with gel. And he was the possessor of a pair of impressive sideburns, and generally rocking a rockabilly style.

"Sir!" said Odelia, calling out to the man. "Can we have a word, please, sir!"

But the man, if he'd heard them, wasn't heeding her call. Instead he kept on walking.

"Sir, Hold up, sir!" Odelia yelled, and made to follow the man. But soon he'd disappeared in the maze of trailers and stalls and the mass of people milling about.

Weird, she thought. He must have heard her.

Then she shrugged. Probably just a coincidence. So she returned to her mom.

Only when she got back to Solange's trailer... Mom was nowhere to be found.

*N*orm was happy. In fact the busily buzzing fly was ecstatic. Not only had he found himself a couple of great new friends but he'd also discovered his purpose in life: to be the bug equivalent of James Bond. A spy fly. Handsome and debonair. In other words a pretty fly fly. And so he'd been practicing his line all morning: 'My name is Fly. Norm the Fly.'

It was a catchy line, and he was pretty sure it would attract a great deal of attention from lady flies. And in fact his wandering eye—all 4500 facets of it—had already spotted just such a deserving lady fly sitting on a shop window, busily cleaning her wings.

She was a shapely fly, he thought—one of those green flies that like to sit on a nice slice of steak, then sit on a pile of cow dung, then sit on a nice piece of cheese, and so on and so forth. Flies like to change things up, and have some variety in their diet, after all.

So Norm now flew in the direction of this lady fly, keen to make her acquaintance, and he was already practicing his line when suddenly he saw a familiar face appear on one of the many television screens lined up behind the shop window: it was none other than Tex Poole, the father of his new friends' human.

"Hey, you guys," he said therefore, for the moment neglecting his role as the new Lothario amongst flies and putting his duty to his newfound friends before carnal desire.

Max and Dooley came trotting up, and were as surprised as he was to see Tex Poole's face reflected in two dozen televisions. Of course Tex Poole's face was also being reflected in Norm's multi-faceted compound eyes but that was neither here nor there.

"Hey, look, Max," said Dooley, the large orange cat's not-so-smart sidekick. "It's Tex."

"Yeah, and Marge," said Max.

And indeed the chunky orange cat wasn't lying: Marge Poole now also featured on the televisions, being interviewed alongside her husband.

"Let's find out what's going on," said Max, and hurried in through the open shop door, followed by Dooley and of course Norm, buzzing right in.

For a moment they sat and watched the interview. It seemed to revolve around a lottery the couple had won, and a cruise they were going to take. Not all that earth-shattering, Norm would have thought, as he wasn't particularly interested in cruises—much too windy for his taste, but Max and Dooley drank it all in. And when next a man was featured named Barry, announcing his upcoming nuptials with a cop named Sarah Flunk, the cats' excitement increased. The interview with the happy couple—though Norm thought the man looked distinctly nervous indeed—was followed by an interview with Wilbur Vickery, the guy whose cat they'd just talked to. Wilbur announced he was now engaged to be married to an actual live princess and would just as soon like to be addressed from now on as Prince Wilbur if it was all the same to his clientele, whom he unfortunately would have to leave soon to take up residence at a castle in England.

Finally the series of interviews concluded with a man named Dan Goory, who looked like Father Time with his long white beard, and whose sole joy in life seemed to be to play with his trains, and especially a very fancy new locomotive he'd just come into the possession of.

By then Norm was already glancing in the direction of that lady fly again, but unfortunately for him she'd taken off, presumably to go sit on some dog poo.

And as they walked out of the shop again, Dooley excitedly said to his friend, "This Madame Solange is amazing, Max. Maybe we should go and pay her a visit. She seems to make everyone's wishes come true!"

"Yeah, she does seem to be some kind of wonder woman," said Max, though he seemed a smidgen less excited than his comrade.

"You don't have a secret wish you would like to see fulfilled, Max?" asked Norm.

"Oh, sure. Lots of wishes. But I'm of the principle that when something looks too good to be true, it generally is. And this Madame Solange looks like such a miracle worker I'm starting to think there's something not completely on the up and up."

"That's because you're a cynic, Max," said Dooley. "And being a cynic is not good for you, you know. You should be open to what life has to offer, and not look a gift cow in the mouth."

"I think the animal you're referring to is a horse, Dooley," said Max.

Dooley thought about this for a moment, then said, "No, definitely a cow, Max."

"I do think maybe we should pay a visit to this Madame Solange," said Max, "but not to ask her to make our wishes come true but to see what's going on. Her name keeps popping up, and I would like to know why."

"Because she's a miracle worker, Max," said Dooley. "Just like you said. And miracle workers should be cherished, not looked upon with suspicion."

"All right, Dooley," said Max. "I promise I'll go in with an open mind, all right?"

"An open mind and an open heart, Max."

"Fine. An open mind and an open heart."

"And let's not forget to keep an open stomach, too," said Norm, who liked to have his priorities straight at all times.

And so it was decided: they'd pay a visit to the fair and learn about the wonders Madame Solange could work for two cats and a fly. At the very least there would be some nice elephant dung to be sampled.

29

*M*arge woke up feeling nauseous and wondering where she was. The room was small but cozily furnished, the couch she was lying on soft and comfortable, but one thing was for sure: she wasn't home. Then she heard a noise and made to get up, only to sink back down again, a dizzy spell forcing her to take it easy.

Finally, when the dizziness subsided, she slowly got into an upright position and glanced out through the window and saw that she was still at the fair: people were walking around outside, and she now figured she'd probably fainted for some reason and some nice folks had put her here to recover.

So where was her daughter? Probably gone to get some professional help, she figured, and so she got to her feet.

And she was just testing her ability to stand upright without toppling over when a dark-haired woman entered the small space and gave her a radiant smile. She closely resembled Madame Solange, only a little older, her face more weathered than Solange's.

"I see you've regained consciousness?" said the woman in a silky voice that sounded very pleasant to Marge's ears.

"What happened?"

"Oh, you passed out," said the woman. "So they brought you here."

"Where is my daughter?"

"She'll be here soon," the woman assured her, and invited her to take a seat again, "before you hurt yourself falling down."

"Thank you so much for this," said Marge, taking a seat as indicated.

"Oh, nonsense," said the woman. "I'm here to help, Marge. So where is your husband? Didn't he join you today?"

Marge wondered how this woman knew she had a husband, but then figured Solange must have told her. "He's at work," she said. "Tex is a doctor," she added for good measure.

"That's nice," said the woman vaguely, and added, "Now let me take a closer look at you, dear. Yes, just look into my eyes for a moment. That's it. There we go..."

Marge didn't know why, but as she gazed into the woman's dark green eyes, she suddenly started feeling very hot indeed, and then before she knew what was happening, she was tumbling down into that same abyss she'd just woken up from. Tumbling and tumbling and tumbling...

❧

"Have you seen my mom?" Odelia asked the guard standing outside Madame Solange's trailer. "She was right there just now, and now she's gone."

"I'm sorry," said the guy, a little gruffly.

"But... did she go off somewhere?"

The bulky man shrugged, and it was obvious he either didn't know or didn't care.

So Odelia decided her mom must have gotten bored waiting for her daughter to return, and must have walked off somewhere to look at some of the other stalls—and there certainly were many of them—dozens or maybe even hundreds—and all of them well-frequented by Hampton Covians having come out in droves for this festive occasion.

Especially kids seemed to be having a ball with the shooting galleries, and the bumper cars and the merry-go-round or even the big Ferris wheel.

So Odelia wandered around a little aimlessly, hoping to bump into her mom again, but when she didn't, took out her phone and tried her mom's cell instead. There was no response, and after a moment Mom's voice invited her to leave a message after the beep.

Weird, she thought with a frown. Mom never neglected to pick up her phone when her daughter called. Could be, of course, that she simply wasn't hearing the ringtone over the din. And soon Odelia found her thoughts returning to the strange events surrounding her uncle's disappearance. First the man was kidnapped from Charlene's home, and now Madame Solange claimed he'd simply taken off to start a new life?

It just didn't make any sense, though of course Solange would say something like that. Odelia wasn't a big believer in fortune tellers, and so she didn't for one minute think Solange was right.

Uncle Alec would never take off like this. Not without talking things through with his nearest and dearest first. Besides, he loved his job, and he loved his new life with Charlene. And though that wedding announcement had been bogus, Odelia wouldn't put it past the couple to tie the knot at some point in the future.

And just when she figured she'd better call it a day and go home, she suddenly thought she saw her uncle's lookalike again: the man was walking not fifty feet in front of her, licking from an ice cream cone and taking in the sights. So this time she decided to play it cool and stalk the man before he skedaddled again.

She didn't think the man's appearance was related to her uncle's disappearance at all, but the resemblance was so uncanny she felt the need to have a little chat with him.

So she carefully trailed the man and soon discovered he was wending his way back to where Madame Solange's trailer was parked. And before she had the chance to talk to him, he'd set foot for a trailer right next to Solange's, and disappeared inside.

For a moment Odelia wavered, then she steeled herself and walked up to the trailer and knocked on the door.

Moments later, the door opened and the man appeared, looking at her a little dumbly.

"Yes?" he said finally.

"Hi, sir,'" said Odelia. "I know this must sound strange to you, but you look so very much like my uncle that I was wondering if perhaps—"

"Your uncle? Who's your uncle?" asked the man, speaking bluntly.

"Alec Lip. He disappeared two days ago, and I've been looking for him, and when I saw you earlier, I just thought..."

"Yes?" said the man, not very invitingly.

She suddenly felt very silly. Plenty of people resembled other people, and just because this man shared a certain resemblance to her uncle didn't mean anything.

"What's your name, sir, if you don't mind my asking?" she said finally.

"Wolf Moonblood," said the man, "and I'm afraid I've never seen you before, miss..."

"Poole," she said, holding out her hand. "Odelia Poole."

"Nice to meet you, Miss Poole," said the man, taking her hand and giving it a quick and unenthusiastic shake. "But I don't think I've ever met this uncle of yours—this Alec Lip. And you say he's gone missing?"

"Yes, he was kidnapped."

"That's too bad," said the man, not displaying much sympathy. "Well, if there's nothing more…"

"No, I'm sorry for taking up your time," said Odelia, feeling exceedingly stupid now and taking a step back.

"Goodbye, Miss Poole," said the man, and withdrew inside the trailer once more.

Odelia stared at the closed door for a moment, and marveled at the striking resemblance both men shared. Though Uncle Alec would never want to be seen dead looking like an aged and much heavier version of John Travolta in Grease.

Then she decided she was wasting her time, and walked away.

Wherever her uncle was, it definitely wasn't here.

"Come on, Brutus," said Harriet. "There has to be someone in this town who knows something."

"I know, but how do we find them?" asked Brutus miserably.

They'd been paying visits to all of their usual haunts but so far had found no one who could shed some light on Uncle Alec's disappearance, or the man with the crooked nose and the cauliflower ears. Usually the modest size of Hampton Cove worked against these crooks and gangsters, as there was always some dog walker or pensioner who'd caught sight of their misdeeds. But not this time.

"We haven't talked to Buster yet," Harriet pointed out. "If anyone can help us, it's him."

Buster was the cat belonging to Fido Siniawski, the hairdresser, and as such usually very well-informed indeed.

Harriet and Brutus walked into Fido's shop, where already plenty of people were waiting to have their hair removed. Harriet had always thought this human habit of allowing other people to mess with their hairdo was one of that particular breed's stranger quirks. She'd never want anyone to touch her nice and perfect fur. Then again, no human could ever hope to have fur as nice and shiny as hers.

"Hey, guys," said Buster when they glanced around to see where the Main Coon was hanging out. "Did you hear the latest? Fido is selling his business and moving to Florida."

"Florida?" asked Harriet, shocked. Fido was such a fixture in Hampton Cove it would be weird to see him leave.

"Yeah, he went to see some woman yesterday, some fortune teller? And she said he'd inherit a winery soon and would go and live in Florida. Now I have to add it's always been Fido's dream to inherit a winery and move to Florida. I think he got it from some movie he once saw, or a book he read. And even though I could have told him that we've got a pretty sweet life up here, of course he wouldn't listen to me."

"Probably because he can't understand a word you say," Brutus pointed out.

"Yeah, there's that, too," Buster admitted. "So this morning, picture my surprise when Fido got a letter in the mail announcing the recent death of some uncle or whatever in Florida, leaving him his winery!"

"Amazing," Harriet marveled.

"This Solange keeps getting it right," said Brutus, equally impressed.

"Yeah, so it looks like it's adieu from me, you guys." Buster sighed. "I'd much rather stay here, though. I like Hampton Cove. And who knows if I'll find friends as nice as you down there in Florida."

"I hear they've got very nice alligators," said Brutus with a grin.

"Yeah, that's not exactly the same."

"Oh, I'll bet they've got cats, too," said Harriet. "There's cats everywhere, Buster. Even in Florida."

"I hope so," said Buster, but he didn't look happy. "You

know the weirdest thing, though? Fido didn't even know he had an uncle in Florida."

"Huh. That is weird," said Harriet.

"So the reason we're here," said Brutus, "is to find out what happened to Chief Alec. He's been kidnapped, and we can't seem to find him."

"Kidnapped! You don't say."

"Yeah, I do say," said Brutus. "So do you have any idea where he might be? Anything you might have overheard or seen?"

The Main Coon thought for a moment, then slowly shook his head. "Nah, I don't think so. In fact this is the first I've heard of this kidnapping business. Fido hasn't mentioned it either, that's for sure."

"Ok, thanks, buddy," said Brutus.

"If you do hear something, let us know," Harriet added, feeling a little dispirited now that even Buster was a bust.

"Oh, sure," said Buster. "And let's get together before I take off for Florida." He smiled a wistful smile. "I don't want to leave before saying goodbye to all of my friends."

"Buster didn't seem happy about the big move, did he?" said Harriet once they'd left the barbershop.

"I don't blame him," said Brutus. "If Odelia suddenly decides to move to Florida I wouldn't be happy either. Leaving all our friends behind."

"Yeah, but that's life, isn't it? Sometimes you just have to go with the flow. And a winery in Florida? I think that would be a great new adventure."

Brutus gave her a curious look. "You're not secretly hoping Odelia wins a winery in Florida, are you?"

"I'm just saying if it did happen, I'd happily go along with it."

"So what now?" asked Brutus, sinking down on his

haunches. They were sitting on the corner of Main Street and Downing Street, and wondering where to go from there.

"I don't know," said Harriet. "I've run out of ideas, snow pea."

"Me, too," said Brutus, glancing around.

Suddenly Harriet saw a man with a funny-looking straw hat across the street and thought he looked familiar. "Hey," she said. "Isn't that Ted Trapper?"

"He looks... happy," said Brutus, referring to their neighbor, the mild-mannered accountant Mr. Trapper.

Ted was coming their way, and as he passed was halted in his tracks by a bald man with bulbous eyes. "Trapper!" said the bald man. "I came to see you at the office and they said you weren't there! What gives, man?"

"I just resigned, Matt," said Ted, a big happy grin on his face. "I quit my job!"

"Quit your job? Are you crazy? A nice steady job like that?"

"We just won the Powerball! One hundred million dollars if you please! We're rich!"

"Well, congratulations," said Matt, shaking the ecstatic ex-accountant's pudgy hand. "Say, could I perhaps trouble you for a small loan?" he asked as both men walked on. "How about a hundred thousand? Or better yet, make that two hundred."

Harriet and Brutus shared a look of surprise. "It's raining lottery winners these days," said Brutus.

"Yeah, looks like," said Harriet. "Hey, watch it!" she yelled when a woman practically stepped on her tail.

"Amazing, isn't it?" said the woman, speaking into her phone while she waited for the lights to turn green. "I just talked to Madame Solange yesterday and today I got word that the adoption papers will be filed next week. We've been waiting two years, Maggie, and all of a sudden it's happening next week!"

The lights did turn green then and the woman walked on, still excitedly chattering into her phone.

Harriet and Brutus shared a look, then nodded. "Let's pay a visit to this Madame Solange," said Harriet, saying what they were both thinking. "We could use a bit of luck."

"*M*ax?"

"Yes, Dooley?"

"If Madame Solange is so smart, maybe she'll be able to talk to us."

"I doubt it, Dooley. It takes a very special skill to talk to cats, and I very much doubt whether Madame Solange possesses that particular skill."

"We can always ask her," Dooley suggested.

Sometimes Max was a little conservative in his views, he thought, and he liked to think it was his task to make him a little more open-minded.

They were staring up at the trailer that appeared to be the home of Madame Solange. A very large man stood sentry in front of the trailer, and looked like the kind of person who brooked no nonsense. As usual, though, he wasn't paying any attention to them, and why would he? Two cats and a fly probably didn't pose a threat to the instructions he was dutifully carrying out.

"I'll bet she can talk to flies," said Norm. "So what say if I go in first and start asking questions?"

146

Flies had such an easy time, Dooley thought. They could just come and go undetected, whereas cats, because of their size, were usually noticed right away.

"Let's stick together," Max now suggested. "It wouldn't do to split up the team now."

"Fair enough," said Norm a little begrudgingly. "So how do you want to play this, Max?"

"We simply slip through the legs of that big man over there, and go and talk to Solange."

"Great idea!" said Dooley, who hadn't thought of that. But then that was why Max was in charge, of course: he always got the best ideas. A kernel of doubt suddenly entered Dooley's mind, though. "What if this big man catches us, Max?"

"Yeah, he looks like the kind of guy who wouldn't mind wringing your necks," said Norm, carefully studying the man, "and stuffing you in his stew."

"Stuff us in his stew!" said Dooley. "He wouldn't!"

"Oh, yeah, he would," said Norm. "Humans eat everything, Dooley, haven't you learned that by now? If it lives and breathes, they don't mind killing it and putting it in their stew."

"But they'd never put us in their stew!" said Dooley, absolutely horrified at the prospect of ending up in the big man's stew tonight. "Besides, we're too hairy. Humans don't like hairy things." He'd witnessed this strange aversion of all things hairy only a couple of days ago, when Odelia had screamed the house down when she caught a hairy spider in the shower. Chase had had to catch it and put it outside.

"I didn't say he'd eat you with hide and hair now did I?" said Norm. "First they skin you and *then* they put you in the stew."

"Oh, no!" said Dooley, starting to panic. "Max! Let's get

147

out of here! I don't want to lose my skin and end up in that
big man's stew!"

"Relax, Dooley," said Max, as usual the epitome of chill.
"No one is ending up in anyone's stew. Not you, not me, and
not Norm."

"Oh, don't you worry about me," said Norm. "Humans
don't eat the likes of me. On the contrary, they can't wait to
get rid of us when they find us floating in their soup."

He was right, Dooley thought. He'd heard the expression
'A fly in the soup' before, and always it was spoken with a
certain distaste. As if flies in the soup were a bad thing.

"Look, I'm sure Madame Solange doesn't eat cats," said
Max, "and neither does her bodyguard, or whatever this guy
is to her. So let's just keep our cool and follow the mission
plan, shall we?"

Dooley nodded, but his mind wasn't at ease as he closely
watched the big muscular man for any signs of cat-eating
behavior. If there was one thing he'd learned about humans
after associating with the species for all of his life, it was that
they were highly unpredictable.

So as they approached the trailer now, and got ready to
slip between the man's legs, Dooley had to really screw up
his courage to the sticking point, and follow Max's lead lest
he chickened out and ran for his life.

But as luck would have it, just then the man was
distracted by a passerby saying hi, and as he was smiling at
the woman, who was very pretty indeed—at least by human
standards—Dooley and Max easily slipped into the trailer
and then they were inside!

"We did it!" said Dooley. "And we didn't get eaten!"

"Or maybe he let you pass, and now you're stuck in here,"
said Norm, ruining the moment with his pessimistic views.

"Let's just go and find this Solange person," Max
suggested, "and we'll worry about the rest later, shall we?"

"Good idea, Max," said Dooley, casting a dark look at Norm, who was already buzzing off to inspect every nook and cranny of the trailer.

They were in some sort of waiting area, where several chairs had been placed. One woman sat waiting there, along with what looked like her daughter, both staring at their phones, and a curtain was hung where presumably Madame Solange held forth.

So they simply slipped through the curtain and then they were in the presence of greatness—or at least the now famous Madame Solange.

From up close and personal she looked even younger than from afar, and not like the kind of fortune tellers Dooley had seen on TV. For one thing she didn't have a hook nose or a wart on the tip of that nose. And she didn't smell of sulfur and camphor either.

"Are you sure this is Madame Solange?" he whispered.

"Yeah, I think so," said Max as they both studied the fortune teller.

She was staring into a crystal ball, and sitting across from an older woman whom they both recognized as Ida Baumgartner, one of Tex Poole's most loyal patients. Ida was intently studying a pot of cream, turning it over in her hands.

"Are you sure this will get rid of my rash?"

"Absolutely," said Solange in melodious tones.

"Mh," said Ida, clearly not convinced. "So can you tell my husband that his Picasso was stolen but then retrieved? Oh, and also tell him that my sciatica is much improved, no thanks to Dr. Poole, who sometimes seems to think I make up these many medical maladies I've been suffering from these last couple of years." She'd opened the little pot of cream, dabbed a stubby finger in and applied some of it to her face, which was indeed very ruddy-looking, Dooley thought. "It doesn't smell very nice," she said critically.

Madame Solange darted a look at Ida that wasn't all that friendly, Dooley thought, but then maybe that was simply her way.

"So if I understand you correctly your greatest wish in life would be for your husband to return from the dead?" said Solange now.

"Of course I know this is quite impossible," said Ida primly, rubbing the cream all over her face now. "Though to be quite honest I don't see why. I mean, they have people frozen and kept on ice until such time as their diseases can be cured, so I keep thinking I should have done the same with my dear, dear Burt."

"I thought you said he died in a car crash?" asked Solange.

"Yes, he did. But still. Future scientists probably will be able to save his life—not the incompetent fools that worked on him at the hospital." She heaved a deep sigh. "Well, at least I can talk to him now, through you, Madame Solange, for which I'm eternally grateful to be sure." She leaned forward. "So has he told you already where he hid that diamond ring he always said he'd buy me?"

Madame Solange's eyes suddenly glittered—a little mischievously, Dooley thought. "What if I tell you that your husband wants to come back to you, Ida? And what if I tell you that maybe—just maybe—he has found a way to do just that?"

Ida seemed taken aback by this. "Burt? Come back to me? But how?"

"Let's just wait and see, shall we?" said the fortune teller, and abruptly placed the doily on top of her crystal ball. "That'll be fifty dollars. And another fifty for the cream."

And as Ida walked out, looking a little discombobulated, Max took this opportunity to jump up onto the chair the woman had vacated and said, "Can I please have a word with you, Madame Solange?"

Dooley held his breath as he watched Madame Solange slowly glance up at Max, then suddenly she frowned and said, "How did you get in here, you filthy creature? Out!"

And to show them that she meant what she said, she got up and made a sweeping motion in Max's direction. "Out, I tell you!" she screamed. "I hate cats—hate them!"

And so Dooley and Max took their leave, hurrying out the same way they'd arrived: by slipping through the legs of that burly guard, who still stood chatting to the pretty young woman.

"I don't think she could understand you, Max," said Dooley once they'd put some distance between themselves and Madame Solange's trailer.

"No, I don't think so either," said Max, panting from both the exertion and the emotion.

Then they both glanced around. "Um…" said Dooley, "so where is Norm?"

Oh, no! They'd left Norm behind! In the hands of that awful Madame Solange!

"We can't just break into her house in broad daylight," said Scarlett.

"Of course we can," said Vesta as she glanced across the street at the house in question.

"You seriously want to break into the Mayor's house right now? When we've only just been released from prison for breaking into Town Hall?"

"Look, you don't have kids, Scarlett, so you don't understand," said Vesta. "But I'd do anything to find my son, even if I find him chopped up and stuffed in Charlene's freezer."

Scarlett pursed her lips. "Well, if you put it that way…"

They were in Vesta's little red Peugeot, parked across the street from the Mayor's house, thinking up ways and means of doing exactly what the neighborhood watch tried to prevent: breaking and entering a house that wasn't theirs.

"Okay, so why don't we simply break a window?" Scarlett suggested now.

Vesta slowly turned to her. "Now you're talking! I like this new and improved Scarlett Canyon."

Scarlett simpered a little. "I just thought of it. I mean, why make things complicated, right?"

"Exactly! And if we get caught we'll simply say we're the neighborhood watch and we were informed burglars were burglarizing Charlene's house and we got there too late to catch the culprits."

"Brilliant!"

"I know," said Vesta, feeling pretty good about her idea herself.

Why she hadn't thought of that last night when they were caught breaking into Town Hall she didn't know. But at least she'd thought of it now. Not that there would be cops around. Not with her son having been 'kidnapped' by kidnappers only Charlene had seen, which told her all she needed to know: the whole story was completely bogus.

"Let's go," she said, and then she and her fellow watch member were darting across the street and making a beeline for the back of Charlene's house. Vesta had brought along the club she'd acquired for watch patrol purposes, and as they arrived on Charlene's terrace, they discovered a wealth of glass they could easily break: there was the sliding glass door, there was the glass kitchen door, and there even was another window that offered a good view of the living room. A regular embarras de richesses!

"So which one do you want to break?" asked Scarlett, eagerly glancing at the large window that led into the living room.

But then Vesta noticed that a window had been left open on the second floor, and she figured that maybe they could manage without causing too much damage for a change.

"If you give me a boost, I think I might be able to reach there," she said, indicating the window.

"Or if *you* give *me* a boost, *I* might be able to reach there," Scarlett countered.

"I thought of it first, so you're boosting me."

"Yeah, but I'm taller so I'll be able to reach that window a lot easier than you."

"Exactly *because* you're taller you'll be able to give me a boost much quicker."

"Okay, fine. Let's toss a coin," said Scarlett.

"Fine. Let's," said Vesta, and took a coin from her purse, then tossed it. The moment it landed, she said, "Heads."

"Hey, no fair—you can't call it after it lands!"

"Who cares! I won so you're boosting me. Let's go!"

"You're impossible, you know that, right?"

"Stop yapping and start boosting already."

So Scarlett got into position and moments later Vesta was reaching for the window.

"You're much heavier than you look!" said Scarlett, groaning under the strain.

"I'm not. You're weak, that's the problem. Now lift me higher, will you?"

"Are you nuts? Do I look like a frickin' weightlifter to you?"

"Higher!"

"Oh, screw this," said Scarlett, and gave one last mighty push. Unfortunately Vesta had just positioned her head underneath the open window and now bumped it against the unyielding object, causing her to let out a sharp cry of pain, then topple down to earth, crashing into Scarlett, and causing the latter to topple over, too.

So when Officer Sarah Flunk rounded the corner ten seconds later, responding to a call from a concerned neighbor who'd witnessed the scene from his balcony window, she found two cursing old ladies trying to extricate themselves from a tangle of limbs.

"Oh, Vesta, Vesta," said Officer Flunk, who was in a great

mood because of her upcoming marriage to Barry Billong, "what is your son going to say when he sees this?"

❧

*N*orm, after his friends Max and Dooley had been kicked out of Solange's trailer, felt it was his duty to stick around, endangering life and limb, to try and complete the mission. It was, after all, what James Bond would have done. Of course James Bond would have tried to seduce Madame Solange and would probably have succeeded, eating up precious minutes of the movie's runtime, but Norm didn't think this was in the cards for him. Women rarely fall for fat flies, except maybe when they look like Jeff Goldblum.

"What did I tell you?" the fortune teller was saying to the muscular guard. "No cats!"

"I'm sorry, Solange," said the security guard. "I didn't see them."

"What am I paying you for, Maxim? To always keep an eye out—even for cats!"

"It won't happen again, Solange," said Maxim ruefully, hanging his head, as far as a neckless man can hang his head, of course. Having been thoroughly chewed out, the guard took his leave and Norm took advantage of this lull in the proceedings to move into another curtained-off area and discover this was Madame Solange's private space.

There was a dresser with a large mirror, and the paraphernalia of a woman's beautifying processes strewn about. He saw several wigs, indicating that Madame Solange liked to change things up as far as her personal appearance was concerned, and also, and most importantly, there were portraits of a certain male bedecking every available surface:

the walls, of course, but also framed pictures festooning the dresser and the little gateleg table next to the small couch and even the TV set where Solange presumably liked to watch some television in between predicting her clients' future.

The male on display wasn't a handsome male but he definitely had Solange's affection: he was a pretty beefy sort of guy, with sideburns and that weird slicked-back coif so popular in the fifties. He sported the same black leather jacket in all the pictures, making Norm suspect he didn't have enough money to buy himself more than one outfit.

Presumably Solange's husband, he thought. He then shrugged and decided to skedaddle. James Bond would have interpreted the fascination of a woman for her own husband as a challenge and would have redoubled his efforts of seduction. James would also have discovered a secret lair underneath the trailer, with a hidden access panel, and he would most probably have been attacked by a one-armed assassin with a gold tooth and a pronounced limp protecting said lair, but then Norm's life was a lot less exciting.

All he'd found were myriad pictures of a rockabilly dude with a weird haircut.

And as he buzzed out through an open window, he hovered over the fairground, gaining some altitude, before buzzing down again when he spotted Max and Dooley.

When he related his recent adventures they were as disappointed as he was.

This investigation wasn't going anywhere fast, that much was obvious. But at least they'd all escaped with their lives, and that was something to be thankful for.

33

As we left the fairground, both Dooley and I feeling a little dejected, we were soon joined by Norm, and as we walked on and he filled us in on what he'd discovered—nothing—we came across two familiar figures in the form of Harriet and Brutus.

"Are you going to see Madame Solange?" I asked. "If so, don't bother." And I told them what we'd found—a cat-hating fortune teller and plenty of pictures of Rockabilly Dude—also known as Wolf, Solange's husband.

Harriet and Brutus both looked a little disappointed by this, and so we soon started our long trek home, to report to Odelia what we'd found—a big, fat nothingburger!

And we would have had only this disappointing news to share if we hadn't suddenly come across a disheveled woman wandering about in the fields that separated the fairground from the first houses of Hampton Cove. For this woman was none other than Marge!

"Marge!" said Dooley.

Marge looked up in surprise. "Oh, hey, Dooley," she said,

giving us a slightly bewildered look. She was missing her shoes, for some reason, and her hair was a mess.

"You're not wearing shoes," said Dooley, observant as usual.

Marge glanced down at her feet as if seeing them for the first time. "You're right," she said after a moment, "and they were new shoes, too." She directed a confused look back at the fairground, whose Ferris wheel and rollercoaster could easily be seen. We could even hear the merry screams of fun of people being jerked around and loving every minute of it. "Um, where am I?" she asked then, a clear sign not everything was as it should be in the world of Marge Poole.

"Did you visit the fair?" I asked, gesturing to the Ferris wheel going round and round.

My human's mom frowned and said, "I think so—I'm not sure." She touched her head, and rubbed it. "My head hurts," she announced.

"So did you lose them?" asked Harriet. "Your shoes?"

"Um… yeah—looks like I did." She frowned some more. "I wonder what happened."

"Let's get you home," Harriet suggested, and started to lead the way in the direction of home and hearth. Marge followed, looking as dazed as I'd ever seen her.

"You know, I think I was going to do something, and then I didn't… I think," she said vaguely, and we all shared a look of concern. Marge clearly wasn't well.

"Did you visit the fairground?" I asked again, hoping to stir a memory.

"Uh-huh. Probably."

"Oh, dear," said Harriet.

And we'd walked a while on a nice asphalt road, which Marge must have enjoyed, for a bare-footed human isn't exactly used to traversing the rough undergrowth us cats are used to navigating, when suddenly a car pulled over and rolled down its window and Odelia's head popped out and she yelled, "Mom! Where have you been!"

And so moments later we were all inside Odelia's pickup, four cats lounging relaxedly in the backseat while Marge took up the front seat, still gazing before her with that slightly dazed look in her eyes.

"What happened?" asked Odelia once she'd put the car in gear and we were tootling along the road into town.

"I... don't know, exactly," said Marge. "I can't seem to recall."

"You remember we went to see Madame Solange, though, right?" said Odelia, looking extremely concerned at the state her mom was in.

"Um... no, I don't think I do." But then Marge's face cleared. "Though now that you mention it... I did visit Madame Solange and she told us we'd win the lottery soon, and go on that nice cruise that Tex is always talking about."

"That was when you and Dad saw Solange, Mom. But you and I paid her visit just now, remember? To ask her about Uncle Alec?"

But Marge slowly shook her head. "No, I don't think I remember that." She glanced over to her daughter. "Are you quite sure that's what happened, honey?"

"Of course I'm sure. We walked out of Solange's trailer and I thought I saw a man who looked like Uncle Alec so I followed him, and then when I got back you were gone!"

"No, I don't think that's what happened," said Marge. "I'm sure I'd remember."

"Marge seems to be completely out of it," said Brutus.

"Yeah, she must have hit her head and is suffering from amnesia," Harriet said.

"Amnesia?" asked Dooley. "Is that lethal?"

"No, amnesia isn't lethal, Dooley," said Harriet. "It's just very annoying."

"Oh," said Dooley, casting a worried glance at Marge, possibly wondering if she was going to die soon now that she was suffering from amnesia.

"Strange things keep happening, don't they?" I said. "With the lottery thing and Marge disappearing and then returning, having lost a chunk of her memory, and Uncle Alec's kidnapping."

"Oh, and you don't even know the best part," said Harriet. "Buster is moving to Florida. Fido inherited his uncle's winery down there."

"And Ted Trapper won a hundred million dollars in the Powerball," said Brutus.

"So weird," I said. "As if a cloud of good fortune has suddenly descended upon Hampton Cove." Or Santa Claus arriving early this year, handing out gifts all over. Only Santa had taken on the form of a woman this time, and her name was Madame Solange.

Just then, Odelia's phone started belting out its ringtone. "Can you pick that up, Mom?" Odelia asked.

Marge took her daughter's phone and picked up, sounding a little hesitant as she said, "This is Marge Poole speaking?" She listened for a moment, then said, "Thank you, sir. I'll tell her," and hung up again.

For a moment, no one spoke, then Odelia asked, "Who was it?"

"Oh, um, a gentleman named Chase Kingsley," said Mom.

"Mom?" said Odelia, glancing over. "You're starting to scare me."

"Why, honey?"

"You honestly don't remember who Chase is?"

"No. Am I supposed to know him?"

"Mom!"

"He said your grandmother has been arrested," said Marge, flicking a piece of fluff from her blouse. "She and Scarlett Canyon were caught trying to break into Charlene's house just now."

"What is happening!" Odelia cried.

I knew just how she felt.

*C*harlene glanced around and for a moment had no idea where she was. Then she remembered. The hospital. Of course. But why? She was feeling fine. In fact she was full of vim and vigor, her energy levels off the charts and ready to hit the road running!

So she practically hopped out of bed and found her clothes neatly folded on a chair in the corner of her hospital room and started getting dressed, humming a tune as she did.

Moments later a nurse walked in and said, alarmed, "Madam Mayor! What do you think you're doing!"

"What does it look like I'm doing? I'm getting out of here," she said good-naturedly.

"But you're not well!" said the nurse.

"Says who?"

"But—"

"Look, I've wasted enough time already, don't you think?" said the Mayor, placing her hands on the nurse's shoulders and giving the woman a reassuring smile. "I have work to do, places to see, people to meet!" And with these words, she walked out, leaving the slack-jawed nurse to stare after her.

Stalking through the squeaky-clean corridors of the hospital, she smiled before herself. She'd never felt this good in her life—what was that silly nurse talking about? And when she fished her phone from her purse and got in touch with her secretary, she barked, "Can you send a car to pick me up at the hospital, Imelda? Thanks!" She was already envisioning great things for Hampton Cove. She would boost the local economy with new projects and a plethora of happenings and festivities. She'd tackle the local housing issue, she'd build a new childcare center—she'd put this town on the map!

She only had to wait five minutes before a car arrived and took her straight to Town Hall, the place where it was all happening! And as she stalked into her office, Imelda got up, a startled look on her face. "Madam Mayor!" she said. "Are you all right? I heard about the hospital and I thought—"

"I'm fine," said Charlene, waving away her secretary's concerns. "Now let's schedule another council meeting, shall we? I have a lot of announcements to make. A lot!"

"But, Madam Mayor…"

"What?" she said, halting in her tracks to shoot her secretary a bewildered look. She didn't understand the woman's reticence. It was almost as if… Imelda had something on her mind. Which of course was impossible. If you worked for a can-do mayor like Charlene Butterwick, only a can-do attitude would do! "Well? Spit it out, woman!"

"I heard about Chief Alec," said Imelda, giving her boss a look of uncertainty. "Is it true? Did the Chief get… taken?"

Charlene frowned. "The Chief? What Chief? What are you talking about?"

"Chief Alec, ma'am. Your… boyfriend?"

"Boyfriend? I don't have a boyfriend, woman. Don't talk

nonsense!" And with these words, she walked into her office and slammed the door. What she really needed, she thought as she took a seat behind her desk, was a new secretary!

🐾

*V*esta and Scarlett didn't have to languish in jail for too long. In fact they didn't have to languish in jail any time at all. Barely had Officer Flunk brought both women in for questioning before Detective Kingsley had taken them off her hands.

"Good luck," said Sarah with a wink, and Chase returned the wink with an eyeroll.

"So what's all this about you two breaking into Charlene's house?" he asked once the two women were seated in front of his desk.

"We weren't breaking in," said Vesta, tilting her chin. "We were merely responding to a report about a man breaking in and so we decided this was just the kind of job the neighborhood watch is designed for."

"Exactly!" said Scarlett.

Chase arched an eyebrow. "You were caught trying to break into a second-story window," he reminded the twosome.

"We were just trying to ascertain whether the burglars had gained access to the property that way," said Vesta stiffly.

"It's what the neighborhood watch does," said Scarlett. "Rescue the helpless! Raise the hopeless!"

"I think that's Captain America, hon," said Vesta.

Chase cleared his throat and placed his phone on the desk, then pressed play on a video displaying the entire scene from the moment Vesta and Scarlett had arrived carrying a large stick, to the moment they'd been arrested and carted off in handcuffs.

For a moment, silence reigned, then Vesta grumbled, "Damn nosy parkers with their damn smartphones. What happened to privacy?"

"Yeah, and the right not to be filmed?" asked Scarlett.

"I think you should sue the person that shot this video," said Vesta, tapping the desk.

"Yeah, I think we should file charges, Vesta."

"Look," said Chase, leaning back. "I get that you're worried about the Chief," he said, "and trust me, I am, too. But this is not the way to find him, all right?"

"But Chase—Charlene's got him!" Vesta cried. "I'm sure of it. She invented this whole home invasion story and in the meantime she's got my son locked up in the basement!"

"Unless she cut him up into little pieces and stuffed him in her freezer," said Scarlett.

"Impossible," said Chase. "And you know why? Because Odelia's cats spent the night at that house, and they didn't find anything. Not a trace of your son."

"Cats aren't infallible," said Vesta. "They could have missed something."

"Also, Harriet and Brutus talked to a dog that lives across the street, and he distinctly remembers three men taking Alec out of the house at the time Charlene says they did. He also offered a very good description of one of the men and of the van they were driving."

This had Vesta and Scarlett stumped for a moment, then Vesta frowned and said, "These men were probably working for Charlene."

"Oh, my God!" said Chase, and dragged his hands through his hair. "Look, Charlene is the victim here, okay? She had nothing to do with this. And if you would just stop barking up the wrong tree, maybe you could actually do something useful for a change and actually help me find your son!"

Vesta gave him a rueful look, and so did Scarlett. "Okay, fine," Vesta said finally. "So what do you think happened?"

"I don't know, but something really weird is going on. I talked to Barry Billong, and he claims a couple of heavies cornered him at work and threatened to break his legs if he didn't propose to Sarah—and Barry had already proposed marriage to another girl."

"I know. He's been cheating on Francine with Sarah for months now," said Scarlett.

"And vice versa," Vesta pointed out.

"So maybe these men did both Sarah and Francine a favor."

"Maybe," said Chase. "But Barry's story unfortunately isn't unique, and I'm not just talking about Alec's kidnapping. People left and right have been winning stuff, or seeing their wildest dreams come true, and it just doesn't add up. Also, I just got a report from the Bridgeport Chief of Police that a valuable model train was stolen from a local collector. He called me because the collector saw that very locomotive appear in a news story." He showed Vesta and Scarlett pictures of the locomotive in question.

"I don't get it," said Vesta. "What are you babbling about, Chase? Just spit it out."

"The same locomotive that was stolen a couple of nights ago turned up last night in the possession of Dan Goory. He claims it arrived on his doorstep. And now I have the unfortunate task of telling him he'll have to hand it back, as it concerns a stolen item."

"So a model train got stolen and turns up in Dan Goory's hands, and Barry Billong was threatened to have his legs broken if he doesn't propose to your officer Sarah Flunk," Vesta summed up the state of affairs. "What has all that got to do with my son?"

"Probably nothing," said Chase, "only your son and Charlene paid a visit to Madame Solange a couple of days before he got snatched, and so did Dan and so did Sarah."

"Huh," said Vesta. "Yeah, looks like you're onto something there, Chase."

"I know," said the cop. "But what?"

Just then, Chase's phone chimed and he saw that Odelia was trying to reach him. "Hey, babe," he said. "If you're worried about your grandmother, I've got her right here."

"That's great. Listen, there's something going on with my mom. I lost her for a while back at the fair, after we paid a visit together to Madame Solange, and the cats found her wandering in the fields and now she's acting really weird."

"Weird, how?"

"For one thing, she doesn't remember who you are."

35

"She looks all right to me," said Tex. He'd briefly examined his wife and now gave her a clean bill of health.

"So why doesn't she remember Chase?" asked Odelia.

We were all in Tex and Marge's kitchen, the entire family having gathered around the kitchen table—minus Uncle Alec, for obvious reasons.

"I'm not sure," said Tex. Then, addressing his wife, "This man over here, honey. You remember him, don't you?"

Marge glanced over to Chase, then smiled and stuck out her hand. "So nice to meet you, sir. What was your name again?"

"Chase," said Chase, a little startled. "Chase Kingsley."

"And you're a cop, Chase?" asked Marge.

"Yes, ma'am, that I am."

"He's also my boyfriend," said Odelia. "Oh, mom, why don't you remember?"

But Marge gave her daughter a curious look. "Remember what, honey?"

Odelia threw up her hands in frustration.

"Do you think Marge remembers us?" asked Dooley.

"Yeah, if she hadn't she would have said so," I pointed out.

"She seems to have lost part of her memory," said Tex. "Though I examined her head and I don't see any evidence of a contusion—no abrasions, bruising or swelling... Could be she suffered a ministroke, but I'd have to take her to the hospital to know for sure."

"She'll get her memory back, though, right?" asked Odelia.

"Hard to say," said Tex. "She might and she mightn't. Memory is a tricky thing."

"Is there other stuff she's forgotten, you think?" asked Vesta. She waved at her daughter. "Marge!" she yelled. "Do you remember me?!"

"She's not deaf," said Tex censoriously.

Marge laughed a careless little laugh. "Of course I remember you, Ma. Don't be silly."

"That's fine," said Vesta, looking satisfied that at least her daughter hadn't forgotten all about her, too.

"She's also completely forgotten about our visit to Madame Solange," Odelia said. "Though not about your visit, Dad."

"Yes, well, like I said, memory loss is a tricky thing, and extremely unpredictable. She might forget something that happened yesterday, and remember something that happened thirty years ago with incredible clarity, or the other way around."

"Listen, honey," said Vesta, patting her granddaughter's knee. "There's something we need to discuss. You better tell them what you told me, Chase," she said.

Chase cleared his throat and opened his notebook. "I would like to read you a brief overview of a number of reports I've received in the last twenty-four hours," he said. "Your boss, Dan Goory, went on television claiming he received a model train, a rare locomotive, in the mail. A train he'd been wanting to lay his hands on for years, right?"

"Yeah, he told me all about it," said Odelia, nodding.

"That particular locomotive was reported stolen from a collector in Bridgeport."

"Dan won't like that," said Odelia.

"There's more," said Vesta. "While Scarlett and I were in Chase's office the reports kept coming in."

"Sarah Flunk went on television announcing her engagement to Barry Billong. Only problem was that Barry has already proposed marriage to another girl, and he was coerced into this second proposal by two men showing up at the dealership and threatening him with physical violence. Wilbur Vickery claims he received a wedding proposal from the daughter of Prince Charles, future king of England. Only problem is that Prince Charles doesn't have a daughter, and the British ambassador, who caught the transmission, has filed an official complaint against Wilbur for making false claims."

"Oh, God," said Odelia.

"Ted Trapper claimed in front of the cameras of an WLBC-9 television crew that he won the Powerball. One hundred million dollars. Only the ticket he received was a fake, and the Powerball has filed charges against Ted for fraudulent claims. Fido Siniawski has testified live on WLBC-9 that he inherited a winery in Florida from his deceased uncle Renny Swaitniki. Only problem is that Renny Swaitniki is alive and well, and not related to Fido, and has now filed charges against Fido for false and hurtful claims. Oh, and a woman named Luella Pear testified in front of WLBC-9's camera that she'd finally been granted adoption of the baby boy she and her husband have been trying to adopt for the past two years. Only the adoption agency have no knowledge about this particular adoption whatsoever and have filed charges against the Pears for false and fraudulent claims." He put down his notebook. "There's more but I think you get the gist."

"And all of these people made these claims after they'd paid a visit to Madame Solange," said Vesta, nodding to Chase.

"Which leads me to think that this Solange just might be behind the whole thing," Chase concluded.

"I like Madame Solange," Marge said chipperly. "She's the kindest, sweetest, most lovely woman I've ever met. And the most generous, too. I think we should invite her."

"Oh, I'm going to invite her," said Chase. "To the police station for an interview."

"I don't like Madame Solange," said Dooley. "She wasn't very nice to us."

"Yeah, she hates cats," I said, taking in what Chase had just said. Clearly Madame Solange was at the heart of some kind of fraud, but what I couldn't figure out was how the whole thing worked, exactly.

Marge patted Chase's knee affectionately. "Are you married, Officer Kingsley?"

"Um, no, ma'am, I'm not," said Chase.

"Why don't I introduce you to Solange? She's a very nice young woman, and I'm sure you and her will get along famously. Do you want me to set it up?"

"Mom!" said Odelia.

"What? I'm just trying to be nice to your friend, honey," said Marge with a shrug. "Spread a little sweetness and light, just like Madame Solange does."

Looked like Solange was spreading more than just sweetness and light, though. She was also spreading a few tactics of wish fulfillment. And I sincerely hoped Chase would get to the bottom of the whole affair.

At least if Marge didn't marry him off to Solange first.

36

"I say we go in there and demand that she give us Uncle Alec back," said Brutus, who's the kind of cat who prefers the heavy-handed approach.

"We can't just go in there and make her do anything," I said. "We're just cats, Brutus. And Solange is a lot bigger and a lot stronger than we are." And if she wasn't, her burly associate definitely was. "Besides, nothing in this whole story tells me that Solange is involved in Uncle Alec's kidnapping."

"Oh, you've got to be kidding me, Max. Of course she's involved!"

"And how do you figure that?"

"What do you mean?"

"Why would a fortune teller abduct a local police chief? Give me one good reason."

"Um…"

"See?"

"I think Chase is wrong," said Harriet. "I think Solange is perfectly innocent of all these crimes he's accusing her of. All I see is a woman who likes to spread a little happiness wherever she goes."

"So how do you explain that a couple of heavies leaned on Barry Billong to make him propose to Officer Flunk?" asked Brutus.

"Probably Sarah's cousins getting sick and tired of her waiting around for this no-good Barry to finally leave his other girlfriend," said Harriet with a shrug.

"And Dan's stolen toy train? And Ted Trapper's fake lottery ticket?"

"I'll bet that Dan Goory arranged the theft of that locomotive himself," said Harriet. "He's been wanting to lay his hands on that thing for so long. You know what collectors are like. Sometimes they go a little berserk."

"And Ted's Powerball ticket?"

"Oh, honey plum. Don't you know by now that people will go to any lengths to get their hands on a little bit of money?"

"Even nice Ted Trapper?"

"Of course! Human nature is what is. They simply can't help themselves, the poor dears."

"Do you think Fido also arranged his so-called inheritance himself?" I asked.

"Of course! Can you imagine having to cut people's hair all your life! I think Fido is probably ready to tear his own hair out by now, and so he made up this entire inheritance story to give himself an excuse to start a new life without people asking him a lot of annoying questions."

"And Wilbur and his princess?"

"Oh, Maxie," she said with a smile. "You know Wilbur. Of course he made the whole thing up. It's just the kind of thing he would do. The man can't get a woman to give him the time of day so now he invents an actual princess to save face in front of his friends and customers." She shrugged. "Like I said, it's all a simple case of human nature. And if you're a keen study of humans, like I am, this is all very easily explained."

"I don't know," I said, not entirely convinced.

"I think you'll find that these people all want something so badly that they'll go to any lengths to get it—even lying and cheating and stealing."

"People are weird," said Dooley, nodding.

"I just wish we could be there when Chase interviews Madame Solange," I said.

"Oh, if you want I'll do the honors," said Norm. "I can be your fly on the wall," he added with a sly little grin.

"Would you, Norm?" I asked. "I'm really curious what she's going to say."

"She'll say the exact same thing I just told you," said Harriet. "Just you wait and see."

Harriet's theory sounded very plausible, but it still didn't explain why Marge had suddenly lost all recollection of who Chase was, or why Uncle Alec was still missing. But of course my friend could be right, and Madame Solange could be absolutely uninvolved in all of these strange occurrences.

I guess we'd soon find out—or at least our resident spy fly Norm would.

§

*N*orm the fly was on a mission again, and this time the mission was even more hairy than his previous ones. He'd been given the order straight from the head of the secret service himself: Max, or, as Norm liked to call him: M.

M had tasked him with a mission to eavesdrop on Chase as he interviewed Solange, and come hell or high water, Norm was going to see this dangerous mission through.

Dangerous because any mission involving humans was

fraught with a certain measure of peril, as humans don't like flies, and enjoy swatting them at any occasion.

But Chase looked like the kind of guy who would stand a fellow a chance, even when that fellow was a fly. And besides, the cop was so preoccupied with his do-or-die interview that he presumably wouldn't even notice the fly observing the proceedings.

So Norm flew on down to the local police station like a bat out of hell, then straight in through the window and took up position in a corner of Chase's office, ready for action.

And he didn't have to wait long, for he'd only just arrived when the suspect was led in. Madame Solange, or Caprice Cooper as her real name apparently was, much to Norm's disappointment, looked almost like a regular person. Gone were the flowing robes, and the low voice, even the smoky makeup. She now looked like any other young woman, one Norm wouldn't give a second glance if he passed her on the street.

Not that he ever gave any human a second glance, unless they came after him with a fly swatter.

"Please take a seat, Miss Cooper," said Chase.

"Mrs. Cooper," the woman corrected him.

"Oh, that's right," said Chase, consulting a file on his desk. "Your husband is Geoff Cooper? Likes to call himself Wolf Moonblood?"

"Yes."

"The owner of Circus Moonblood."

Mrs. Cooper nodded, and glanced around a little uncomfortably. "So why am I here?"

"The thing is, Mrs. Cooper, that a number of complaints have been made."

"Complaints? About me?"

"I'll just run down the list, shall I? And you can tell me what you think." And Chase read out the entire list of strange occurrences that had taken place of late, and stressed that each time the people it happened to had previously visited Madame Solange.

Solange shrugged. "I don't know anything about that, Detective. Basically I just tell people what they want to hear, and they pay me very handsomely for the privilege."

Chase sat back. "So you tell the people what they want to hear…"

"Yep. That's my big trade secret. I hope you won't blab about it," she added with a half-smile.

"But… so how do you explain that people actually get what they want… but in evidently fraudulent ways?"

"No idea. I guess you'd have to ask them."

"Take Dan Goory for instance," said Chase. "He wants a certain model train, he tells you he wants this model train, you tell him he'll *get* his model train, and a couple of days later it arrives on his doorstep… stolen from a collector in Bridgeport. How do you explain that?"

"Simple. Mr. Goory wanted that train so badly he stole it. And now he's blaming me."

"Have you been to Bridgeport lately, Mrs. Cooper?"

"Nope. I've been right here in Hampton Cove since I arrived in town a week ago."

"Where were you on the evening of the fifteenth at ten o'clock?"

"Like I said, I haven't left town since I arrived—me and my husband."

"Mr. Russ Mulling, the collector of this very valuable locomotive, claims to have been the victim of a burglary on that particular night. He even got a snapshot of one of the thieves." The cop placed a picture in front of Madame Solange, who glanced at it without much interest.

Norm, who liked to do things properly, buzzed down

from his hiding place, and did a quick flyby to get a closer look. M would want him to memorize all the details.

Madame Solange, or Caprice Cooper, frowned at him and even made to swat him! Luckily he was a trained spy fly, and managed to escape unscathed. The man in the picture was very large, had a crooked nose and cauliflower ears, and looked like a boxer. He also looked exactly like one of the three men who'd abducted Uncle Alec!

"I've never seen this man before in my life," now said Solange.

"Or what about this man?" said Chase, and placed another picture next to the first one. "He was caught on CCTV leaving the Toyota dealership where Barry Billong works, after threatening Barry that he'd break his legs, arms and neck if he didn't propose marriage to my colleague Officer Sarah Flunk."

Once again Norm did a flyby, and this time he saw that this second man was the same man as the first man, the knowledge of which would have saved him a dangerous stunt, as once again Solange tried to slay him with a swatting motion of her hand!

"Like I said, I don't know this man, have never seen this man, and have no idea why he would do such a thing," said the fortune teller.

"Look, I'll be blunt with you, Mrs. Cooper," said Chase.

"I thought you already were being blunt, Detective Kingsley," said the woman with a smile. She was charming, Norm thought. Very charming—and potentially deadly!

"You promise people the world, and then all of a sudden, and seemingly out of the blue, people get exactly what they asked for. Only it's not the hand of Lady Luck making their dreams come true but this man and his associates. So that leads me to think—"

"That I run some kind of wish-fulfillment racket? Why

would I do that, Detective? Why would I risk going to prison just to collect a measly fifty bucks from my clients? You'll have to admit that doesn't make any sense."

Chase stared her down for a moment, but Solange easily held his gaze.

"All right," said Chase finally. "You can go. But I'll be watching you, Mrs. Cooper. And if I find that you do know these people, I will find you."

"Oh, please do, Detective," said Solange, her voice almost a purr. "In fact I hope you do drop by sometime. I'm sure there are things you wish for that I could easily make come true." And with these words, which practically amounted to a gauntlet being thrown down, wrapped in flirtatiousness, she walked out.

The moment she had, Chase glanced up at Norm. "Did you get all that, buddy?"

"Oh, yes, Chase, thank you," said Norm, pleasantly surprised at this acknowledgment.

The cop shook his head. "I can't believe I'm talking to a fly. I must be losing it."

37

The four of us had decided to stick close to Marge. Obviously the poor woman wasn't well, and it behooved us, as the family pets, to keep an eye on her.

She was seated on the couch, watching the Kardashians, and laughing loudly in all the wrong places, while her husband kept darting anxious glances in his wife's direction.

Vesta was also there, though she seemed less worried about the whole thing. But then Gran is a tough old bird, and probably has been through a lot worse than her daughter forgetting a few minor details about her life, such as the entire existence of Odelia's boyfriend.

And it was as we were watching the shenanigans of Calabasas's first family that Norm came buzzing in, and we all turned to him, eager for some news from the front lines.

"She didn't do it," he said immediately. "No motive."

"Oh," I said, deflating a little.

"Yeah, Chase grilled her pretty hard, but she didn't crack. Did you know, by the way, that Solange isn't her real name? She's really called Caprice Cooper, and she's a lot plainer-looking without all that makeup and those funky witch's robes."

"Great," said Brutus. "So now we have a crime but no suspect. What are we going to do?"

"I have no idea," I said.

"Honey?" said Marge all of a sudden.

"Yes, sweetheart?" said her husband.

"Did we always have this many cats?"

"Oh, for crying out loud!" said Gran. "Don't tell me now you can't remember our cats!"

"Oh, I remember we had one—but four? That seems like an awful lot of cats, don't you think?"

"Which one do you remember?" asked Tex.

"Well, that pretty white one, of course. Her name is Princess, right?" She waved at Harriet. "Hi, Princess. You're a real cutie pie, aren't you? Sweet, sweet Princess."

Dooley turned to me with a look of alarm. "Max, Marge has forgotten us—she's totally forgotten we even exist!"

"Yeah, it certainly looks that way," I agreed, studying the forgetful woman closely. She was looking far too chipper, I thought. As if she was high on some unknown substance.

"Marge, that pretty white cat's name isn't Princess, it's Harriet," said Tex slowly.

"Are you sure?" said Marge. "I could have sworn her name was Princess. She certainly looks like a Princess to me."

"No, definitely Harriet," said Tex.

"Though I like the name Princess, too," said Harriet now, preening a little.

Marge stared at Harriet. "So sweet." She patted 'Princess' on the head, then returned her attention to the reality show blaring away on TV.

Gran gave her daughter a look of alarm. "Marge? Don't tell me you can't understand what Harriet just said."

Marge looked up with a sweet smile. "Mh?"

"Harriet, say something," Gran instructed.

"What do you want me to say?" asked Harriet.

"Ask Marge to name the capital of China."

"I don't even know what the capital of China is."

"Just do it, will you?"

Harriet sighed. "Marge, what is the capital of China?"

But from Marge there was no response. Gran groaned. "I knew this would happen."

"Honey, did you hear what Harriet just said?" said Tex.

Marge laughed. "But, sweetie, how can I understand Princess? You know cats can't talk. And now please let me watch the show. I like it. It's very entertaining."

Now we all shared a look of alarm. "She was able to understand us before," I told Gran. "I mean, when we found her wandering in the fields she talked to us just fine."

"It's her mustache," said Gran. "Scarlett warned me that if you let those hairs grow unrestrained they will affect your brain."

And then she abruptly rose from the couch and stalked out of the room. Moments later we heard her stomp up the stairs.

"Gran is clearly upset," said Dooley. "She's probably gone off to cry in her room."

"Yeah, can you blame her?" asked Brutus. "Marge doesn't remember us—and she can't talk to us anymore either. This is a nightmare."

"Can a ministroke do so much damage?" asked Dooley.

"Yeah, looks like," I said.

"So maybe she should have another ministroke?" Brutus suggested. "That way she'll snap out of it. We could knock her on the head, for instance. I'll bet that would do it."

"I don't think it's that simple," I said. "Brain trauma and memory loss are very tricky things. Tex said so himself."

We all stared at Tex, who sat staring dumbly at his wife,

who sat staring gleefully at Khloé Kardashian complaining about her complexion.

It was a surreal scene, to say the least.

Moments later Odelia walked in, followed by Chase, and they both had that glum look on their faces that spoke of an investigation stuck in the doldrums.

"And?" said Tex hopefully. "Did you make an arrest?"

"Nope," said Chase. "No motive to speak of, and nothing that directly links her to the string of fraudulent claims. I am going back to the fair tomorrow. Dig a little deeper."

"I'm also going, and so are you guys," said Odelia, addressing us.

"Can I come, too?" asked Norm excitedly. "I feel like I'm on a real streak here."

"Sure you can come," I said. "In fact we couldn't do this without you, Norm."

Norm glowed with pride, as far as a fly who's not a firefly can glow, of course.

"So there's been a complication," said Tex. "Your mother doesn't seem to remember the cats, except for Harriet, who she thinks is called Princess. She's also forgotten she can talk to her cats, which is a bad sign."

"Oh, dear," said Odelia, sinking down next to her mom and rubbing her back.

Marge gave her daughter a radiant smile. "I like these Kardashians," she said. "Is this a new show? I hope they keep it going. It's very funny."

"It's been on TV for years, Mom," said Odelia. "And what is this about you not being able to talk to our cats?"

"Talk to our cats!" said Marge with a tinkling laugh. "Honey, you really have to stop pulling my leg. You know I'm not well—or at least your father seems to think so."

"Oh, Mom," said Odelia, casting a look of concern at her boyfriend.

"Oh, hi, dear," said Marge, noticing Chase. "So did you and Solange go on a date?"

"Yeah," said Chase after a moment's hesitation. "Yeah, I guess you could say that."

"And did sparks fly?" asked Marge with a cheeky smile.

"Oh, sparks flew, all right," said the cop.

"Good. That girl deserves to be happy. She lost her husband, you know. Sad case."

"Did Solange lose her husband?" asked Odelia.

"No, she assured me her husband is alive and well," said Chase.

"I met him," said Odelia, nodding. "Though I didn't know he was her husband."

"Yeah, he runs the circus. According to what I could find out they've been married for years. Though it's hard to be sure, as records are a little sketchy on both Mr. and Mrs. Cooper—seeing as how they travel around a lot."

Just then, Gran came stomping down the stairs again, holding some mysterious object in her hand. And before we knew what was happening, she'd glued a strip of something under her daughter's nose, then said, "This hurts me more than it hurts you, honey, but it's for your own good!"

And then she yanked the strip off, causing Marge to screech out a loud cry, and Tex yelling, "What do you think you're doing?!"

"Waxing her mustache!" Gran held up the strip, now containing lots of minuscule hairs, while Marge sat rubbing her upper lip and giving her mom a look of horror. "Your memory will start coming back now, honey," said Gran, patting her daughter's head. "It's the hairs, you see. They grow straight into your brain and make you forget stuff."

"Oh, I'll make *you* forget stuff!" said Marge, and lunged for her dear old mother, who expertly managed to dodge this attack.

And soon Marge was chasing her mom around the family room, with Gran waving that strip of waxing paper like a banner.

"This is fun," said Norm. "Is this the way you guys spend all your evenings?"

*T*ex wasn't exactly feeling on top of the world when he walked into the New York Lottery Customer Service Center the next morning. There was a line of people waiting as he settled in at the back, holding his winning ticket in his hand. His plan was to cash in and head straight to the travel agent to book that Caribbean cruise for him and Marge.

Marge might be suffering from severe memory loss now, but once she was aboard that fine and luxurious vessel and cruising along the Caribbean, he hoped that bracing ocean air would do her good, as well as being away from Hampton Cove for a while.

The door opened again and a familiar figure walked in and joined the line.

"Oh, hi, Charlene," he said. "How are you holding up?"

The Mayor frowned and sized him up as if she'd never seen him before in her life, then said, "Tex Poole, isn't it? Doctor Tex Poole? I never forget a face."

Tex laughed a light laugh. "Very funny, Charlene."

"Why do you keep calling me Charlene? It's Madam Mayor to you, Dr. Poole."

"But..."

"Look, I know there's this tendency nowadays to call public servants by their Christian name, probably exacerbated by social media and its pernicious influence, but I for one am absolutely against that sort of familiarity. I worked hard to become Mayor of this town, and I think I deserve the respect that comes with the job, Dr. Poole."

"Oh, sure," said Tex, wondering if the whole world had gone stark raving mad.

"Now please tell me, Doctor. Is this where I can buy tickets for the Bruce Springsteen concert?"

"Bruce Springsteen?"

"I'm a big fan of Bruce Springsteen, and I just have to get tickets for his next show."

"This is the claim center for the New York Lottery," said Tex, choosing his words carefully, lest Mayor Butterwick suddenly stage an attack on his person—she looked a little manic, he thought.

"Lottery?"

"Yep," he said, pointing to a large banner that said, 'New York Lottery—We Always Go For Your Win!'

"Oh," said Charlene, then seemed to give herself a little shake. "Then I guess I made a boo-boo," she said, and promptly walked out again.

And Tex was still thinking about this strange conversation with Charlene when it was his turn to turn in his ticket. The woman behind the counter gave him a welcoming smile, indicating she was there to go for his win, and scanned his ticket in her little scanning gizmo. Her smile faltered when the results of the scan appeared on her screen.

"Is something wrong?" asked Tex.

"Where did you get this ticket, sir?" she asked.

"I bought it at the General Store," he lied through his teeth.

The woman gave him a quick glance, then seemed to press a button underneath her desk. "I'm afraid there's been some kind of mistake, sir. This ticket is a forgery."

"A what?" he asked, aghast.

The woman nodded, then darted a look behind Tex. And when he turned, he saw they'd been joined by two very buff-looking gentlemen, who didn't look like they were going to do whatever it took for Tex to get his win.

ֆ❧

*C*hase was on his way to the station when he got the call. "Yeah, Dolores," he said, after pressing a button to activate his wireless headphones so he didn't have to take his hands off the steering wheel. "Shoot. But not with live ammo, please."

And he was still smiling at his corny joke when Dolores's raspy voice announced, "Just got a call from the lottery office, sweetie. Looks like your future father-in-law was just caught trying to cash in on a forged lottery ticket."

"Oh, God," he said, and promptly made a U-turn.

"No, still Dolores," said the station dispatcher, now chuckling at her own corny joke. "Maybe it would save us time if you just went and arrested your entire family, Chase," she added. "We already booked Vesta yesterday, now it's Tex's turn, so I'm just wondering when we'll have to haul in Odelia and her mom."

"Very funny, Dolores," he grunted, squeezing that accelerator closer to the metal.

"I knew I should have become a standup comedian," she said and disconnected.

Moments later he was parked in front of the lottery office

and heading inside. After introducing himself to the lady at the desk, he was buzzed into the office behind her, and the scene he found next was a little disconcerting: there Tex Poole sat, two very large security guys hovering over him, the good doctor looking very embarrassed indeed.

"I didn't do it, Chase!" said Tex. "I didn't doctor a fake lottery ticket!"

"I'll take it from here, shall I?" Chase suggested, and escorted the doctor out of the office.

"I don't know what's going on," said Tex once they were outside. "First Alec is abducted, then Marge loses her marbles, and now I'm arrested—am I under arrest, Chase?"

"No, you're not," said Chase. "Though the New York Lottery might press charges so it wouldn't be a bad idea to call your lawyer."

"Word will spread," said Tex miserably, "and my patients will think I'm a cheat and a fraud. How am I ever going to face them?"

"Just tell them what you told me. That you're not a fraud. Do you still have the envelope the ticket came in?"

"No, I threw it away."

"Can I see the ticket?"

Tex handed him the ticket in question.

"Looks genuine," said Chase, studying the winning lottery ticket that should have netted Tex fifty thousand smackeroos but had instead landed him in hot water—and not the Caribbean kind either.

"It's a fake," said Tex. "Those guys in there? They told me it's not even a good fake. They say people try to defraud the lottery all the time, and as far as fakes go, they've seen it all, and this one looks like it was made by a ten-year-old." He sighed. "So even as a fraud I'm a total failure."

Chase placed his hand on the doctor's shoulder. "Don't

sweat it, Dad. I'm going to get to the bottom of this thing, and when I do, we'll be able to clear your name, all right?"

Tex nodded. "These are strange times we live in, Chase. I just saw Charlene in there, and she didn't even know who I was. Can you believe it? Looks like she lost her memory, too —just like Marge did."

And as Chase watched the doctor walk down the street, on his way to his office, his shoulders stooped and looking distinctly dejected, the cop figured now was as good a time as ever to follow up with the Mayor.

39

*C*harlene Butterwick was busy at her desk when Chase walked in.

"Yes, yes, YES!" the mayor practically screamed, which caused the cop to raise one eyebrow incrementally and wonder if perhaps the doctors at the hospital had discharged the burgomaster a little early.

"Hi, Charlene," he said warmly. "Just thought I'd drop by to give you an update on the investigation."

"What investigation?" said the Mayor, turning a feverish eye on him. "WHAT INVESTIGATION!"

"Um, the one about the home invasion?"

She stared at him as if he'd lost his mind. "WHAT HOME INVASION!" she screamed, and suddenly picked up a small bust of the previous mayor and threw it at his head!

Chase expertly ducked the bust, and watched it crash against the wall behind him.

"Are you sure you're all right, Charlene?" he asked. "You look a little... stressed."

"What's with people calling me Charlene!" she said. "It's

MADAM MAYOR to you, sir. MADAM MAYOR to all! And who are you?"

"Chase… Kingsley?" he said, starting to recognize the same signs Odelia's mom was displaying. "Detective Kingsley," he added, figuring that maybe using his official title would protect him from more busts being aimed at his noggin.

"DETECTIVE Kingsley," said Charlene between gritted teeth. "Look at me. I'm a professional woman with a very, VERY busy schedule. So why did you think it was a good idea to BOTHER ME WITH THIS NONSENSE!"

"But—"

"GET OUT!"

"But Madam Mayor!"

"OUT!" she screamed, and lifted up a slightly heavier version of the first bust. Before she could throw it, though, he'd already followed her advice and hurried out of the office.

There was a dull clunking sound when the bust hit the closed door behind him, and a loud scream of frustration and then all was quiet again.

Chase cocked an inquisitive eyebrow at Charlene's secretary Imelda, who gave him a distraught look.

"She's not herself, Detective," said the woman, stating the obvious. "I don't think she even remembers who I am anymore. One moment she calls me Mildred, the other Deirdre. And she keeps telling me to gather the troops for an emergency meeting. I figured she meant the council members, but I really can't expose her to their scrutiny when she's behaving like this. They'll have her carted off to the nearest loony bin!"

"I think she probably needs to see a professional," Chase agreed. "She never should have been discharged so quickly."

"Oh, but physically she's perfectly fine," said Imelda.

"She's got the strength of an ox. Only this morning she threw a bust of Mayor Moss through the window that must have weighed at least thirty pounds. It narrowly missed the head of one of the gardeners."

"She threw a bust at me, too," said Chase. "Two, even."

"Maybe she should pursue a career in basketball when politics doesn't pan out," Charlene's loyal secretary said, darting a worried look at the door of her employer.

༖

*F*ather Reilly gave the cord attached to one of the bells in the church bell tower an extra vigorous pull, making it spread its sound far and wide and inviting parishioners to join the priest for mass. Very soon now the church would not only have the new roof he'd been pestering anyone who would listen about, but a brand-new set of bells, too!

So it was with a swing in his step that the white-haired priest now set foot for his office, where he'd been working on a jubilant sermon to rival the Pope's Easter homily.

Father Reilly wasn't usually the kind of person to believe in fortune tellers or psychics or tarot readers or people of that ilk, but he'd been seduced to the dark side when one of his parishioners had returned from a visit to Madame Solange and had sang that talented woman's praises. This particular parishioner had suffered from a very stubborn form of toe fungus and Madame Solange had told him that very soon now he'd come into the possession of a cream that would clear up that fungus once and for all.

And lo and behold, the very next day just such a cream had found its way into his possession in the form of a UPS delivery, and the first results were promising indeed.

So Father Reilly had momentarily suspended his disbelief

and had paid a visit to the wondrous world of Madame Solange. The woman, after gazing intently at her crystal ball, had told him a new church roof would soon materialize, as well as a new set of bells for his bell tower, and so it was with a sense of anticipatory glee that the priest now opened his laptop and added a few more phrases to his latest sermon—a real scorcher!

"Jesus wants the best for each of us, and so nothing but the best is what each of us should expect," he murmured as he deftly stabbed at the keyboard in his usual hunt-and-peck approach to typing.

Just then, a messenger suddenly appeared in the door, looking bored. "Package for Francis Reilly—please sign here," the messenger intoned in a monotone, and held out a stylus for Father Reilly to use. After having jotted down a scribbled affirmation that he was, indeed, Francis Reilly, the priest eagerly began unwrapping the package. It couldn't be a new church roof, as usually church roofs are a little bigger than the five-pound package that was now on his desk. But it could be a bundle of cash, or a sheaf of checks.

But when finally he'd opened the package, he found that it contained a set of bells—very, very small ones.

He sank back on his chair as he stared at them.

But before he could wonder who was playing this cruel joke on him, suddenly two more people appeared in his office, this duo hoisting a microphone and a camera.

And as he glanced up, still struggling to contain his disappointment, the one with the microphone asked, "So did your wish come true, Father Reilly? Did Madame Solange work her miracles again?"

He would have thrown them out on their ear, or given them a piece of his mind, but a good Christian doesn't let his anger get the better of him, and so he said, in measured tones, "I think there's been some kind of mistake."

40

$\mathcal{U}$ sually when people announce that they're going to spend a fun day at the fair, this is greeted with loud cheers and happy faces all around. When Odelia had told us last night that she wanted us to join her at the fair, only grim faces set with resolute looks of determination greeted her announcement.

It had, after all, been one of those weeks, where tragedy meets misery, and bumps shoulders with terrible misfortune.

For a short rundown I'd like to remind you that this was the week Uncle Alec had been kidnapped, Marge Poole had lost her mind, Tex Poole had been accused of lottery fraud, Charlene Butterwick had gone cuckoo, Gran had been arrested numerous times, Dan Goory had been accused of theft, Sarah Flunk had been proposed marriage by a car salesman and wannabe bigamist under duress, Wilbur Vickery had been accused of lies and deceit by the British royal family, Fido Siniawski had been accused of deceit by an uncle who wasn't even his uncle, and I'm probably forgetting a host of other stuff.

All in all, it had been a pretty eventful couple of days for

194

Hampton Covians, and it all seemed to be connected to the fair in some way that Odelia vowed to figure out before the day was through.

Lucky for us, we had a powerful ally in Norm, or Buzzing Bond as he was now calling himself. So it wasn't without a certain sense of hope that we piled into Odelia's aged pickup, and made the trip down to the fair.

"So you guys spread out and try to pick up some of the chatter, all right?" said Odelia, giving us some of those last-minute instructions any good coach knows mean the difference between winning or losing.

"Yes, Odelia," said Dooley dutifully.

"Meanwhile I'll go and have another word with Madame Solange. There simply has to be a connection between what she claims to see in that crystal ball of hers and what's been happening to the people of this town."

"Do you think she's a witch?" asked Harriet now, introducing an interesting new theory.

"I'm sorry, Harriet, but witches don't exist," said Odelia with a smile.

"But... how about Harry Potter?" asked Dooley, looking disappointed. "Doesn't Harry Potter exist?"

"Harry Potter is fiction, Dooley," said Odelia. "He's not real, and neither is the world of wizardry described in those books."

"Are you sure?" my friend asked, looking stricken by this revelation.

"Yes, I'm sure," said Odelia. Her smile then was replaced with the look of determination that had been there before. This was clearly a woman on a mission—a mission to find her missing uncle, and her mother's missing memory.

"I just hope that we won't lose our memory, too," said Brutus, striking the morbid note. He turned to Harriet. "If I forget who you are, honey bunny, I just want you to know that the last couple of months have been the best years of my life."

"Oh, that's so sweet of you, honey plum," said Harriet. "But don't worry about losing your mind. If you forget who I am I'll simply hit you over the head until you remember."

Brutus gulped a little at this, and I think it was safe to say he swore a solemn oath right then and there never to lose his memory.

"Chase just called," said Odelia as she cruised along the small roads that traverse the fields surrounding Hampton Cove. "My dad tried to cash in his fifty-thousand-dollar lottery ticket and was almost arrested for fraud. Turns out the ticket was a fake, and now they're considering pressing charges against him. And Chase was chased out of Charlene's office—he says she doesn't remember who he is." She sighed. "Things just keep getting worse and worse, don't they?"

"You'll figure it out," I assured my human. "And we'll help you as much as we can." I was drawing the line at entering Madame Solange's trailer, though. The woman was a cat hater, and there was no telling what she might do when she laid eyes on us again.

"So what is my mission, M?" asked Norm.

"Your mission, if you choose to accept it," I said with a smile at the industrious fly, "is to sneak into Solange's trailer once more and try to find out as much as you can about her operation. There must be something we're missing, Norm. There just has to be."

"Aye, aye, sir," said the fly. "One more question if I may, sir?"

"Shoot, Norm," I said, perhaps a little injudiciously.

He dropped his voice an octave, to indicate the gravity of his request. "Do I have a license to kill?"

"Yes, you do," I said, just as gravely. Extreme situations demand extreme measures, and even though I didn't believe in executive force, as far as I was concerned we needed to go to any lengths now to find Uncle Alec and restore law and order in our small town.

"So what are you going to do, Norm?" asked Brutus. "Kill your target by buzzing them?"

"Oh, don't you worry about me, Brutus," said Norm, swelling up a little from sheer self-importance. "Agent Buzzing Bond always hits his target."

"Oh, boy," said Harriet, shaking her head. "Sometimes I feel like I've landed in the middle of a vaudeville act. And a pretty lame one, too."

"I think it's great that Norm is offering to help us," said Dooley. "We need all the help we can get on this one."

"Rightly spoken, Dooley," I said.

"I feel like we're up against a formidable enemy," my friend continued. "An enemy whose name just might begin with Volde and end with Mort, if you see what I mean."

"Oh, Lord," Harriet groaned. "Please kill me now."

"I could, if I wanted to," said Norm seriously. "But even though I now have a license to kill, I like to use it with extreme caution, so you're off the hook, Harriet."

For a moment I thought Harriet would use her license to kill to swat Norm, but she restrained herself with an extreme effort, restricting herself to giving me a very dirty look indeed. It was obvious what this look said: when this is over, that fly's ass is grass.

41

*S*olange, when she entered her trailer, was surprised to find her husband of fifteen years gazing steadily out the window, staring at nothing in particular.

"Wolf, honey," she said. "Are you all right?"

Wolf turned. "Mh?" he said. "Oh, sure. Fine, fine." Then he frowned. "It's just that…"

"More strange dreams?"

"Yeah, I guess you could say that. I dreamt last night that I was a cop." He chuckled at this. "Can you imagine? Me! A cop!"

Solange gave her partner a look of concern. "You know what you should do? Go and have a long talk with Selena. Like you promised you would."

"I don't want to talk to your sister," said Wolf, his smile vanishing. "Every time I talk to her I end up with a splitting headache."

"That's because you fight her," said Solange. "If you'd simply go along with her and do what she says, you would be just fine."

Wolf's face had taken on the mulish look she'd seen there

so often these last couple of days. "I don't think I like your sister. She always looks at me funny."

"Funny, how?"

"Like… she thinks I'm not firing on all cylinders or something."

"No, she doesn't. She's just concerned about you, that's all. Like we all are."

"Are *you* concerned about me?" asked her husband, now turning away from the window and giving her a quizzical look.

"Of course I am. You've been behaving really strangely, honey. You know you have."

"It's these dreams," he muttered, and patted his gelled hair, which soon looked like a bundle of porcupine quills sticking in every direction. "These dreams I've been having."

"Stop touching your hair," she said, annoyed.

"I like touching my hair. It makes me feel good."

"I just wish you'd stop. You'll ruin your perfect coif."

He nodded obediently and heaved a deep sigh. "I'll go and see your sister."

"Thank you," said Solange, much relieved. "You'll feel much better once you do."

"I wonder, though…" said Wolf with a frown.

"Yes?"

He stared at her for a moment. "A woman came to see me yesterday. She said her name was Odelia Poole. She's a reporter."

Solange's expression darkened. "Yes, and?"

"Somehow she looked… familiar. Though for the life of me I can't seem to place her."

"Then don't. She's just a nosy parker—snooping around and asking a lot of annoying questions." Not for the first time Solange felt they probably should shake Hampton Cove's dust off their feet. In their line of work overstaying their welcome usually led to trouble. "If she comes back, just let the boys handle her, all right?"

"All right," said Wolf vaguely.

She walked up to her husband and planted a gentle kiss on his lips. "Promise me," she said, fixing him with an intent look.

"She's just a reporter, sweetie. I can handle reporters."

"Promise me," she insisted when he tried to avoid her gaze.

"Okay, okay, I promise. I don't see what the big deal is anyway."

"Trust me, it's important," she said, placing her hands on his sideburns. "You're going to need another touch-up soon," she announced with a smile. "After you've talked to Selena," she quickly added.

"Oh, all right," said her reluctant husband.

&

Odelia met Chase in the fairground parking lot. The cop had brought a couple of colleagues, and they'd already drawn up their plan of campaign: Chase had finally decided that there was no use hiding the truth from his fellow officers any longer, and had gathered them together in the police precinct main office that morning after returning from his visit to Charlene, and told them that Alec Lip, their beloved boss and chief, had been abducted.

Since the kidnappers hadn't been in touch since the abduction, it was safe to assume that their demand that the news of his abduction remain a secret was now null and void.

So this had officially become a rescue mission, and the main investigation Chase and the rest of the Hampton Cove Police Department would pursue from now on.

"Do you really think Uncle Alec is being held here somewhere?" asked Odelia.

"I have no idea, babe," said Chase. "But I'm willing to bet my badge that he is. And if we find this guy," he added, holding up a picture of the man with the crooked nose and the cauliflower ears, "we'll be much closer to the truth." He'd distributed the picture among his officers, and he'd vowed to leave no stone unturned to find the guy today.

"I want to have another word with Solange," said Odelia. "Though I doubt whether she knows anything. I'm starting to think someone is using her to set up some kind of scam operation."

"Which begs the question: what do they hope to gain from making people's wishes come true? Solange was right: for a measly fifty bucks she promises people all kinds of things, so where is the benefit?"

She patted her boyfriend's chest. "I'm sure you'll find out, Detective."

"All right, people!" Chase yelled to his collected colleagues. "Let's do this!"

And thus Operation Save Chief Alec was finally underway—officially this time.

❧

The fairground was buzzing with activity. It wasn't just a fair, but also a circus, and since Madame Solange and her cohorts were part of the circus setup, and circuses, as far as I'd ascertained from extensive research—all the hours spent watching movies and television shows—employ at any given time any number of heavily built men, possibly outfitted with crooked noses and cauliflower ears, I decided this should be our focus.

So it was with a certain measure of resolve that Dooley

and I headed that way, while Brutus and Harriet, who had other opinions on how to run an investigation, went the other way, vowing to take a closer look at some of the other attractions, such as there were a hot dog stand, a funnel cake stand, a cotton candy stand, a deep-fried Twinkie stand, an ice cream stand, a jalapeno popper stand, a fried chicken stand, a lobster corn dog stand... In other words: Brutus was probably hungry, and so was Harriet.

"Do you know I've never been to the circus, Max," said Dooley as we approached the area where the large and potentially dangerous circus animals were kept—the man with the cauliflower ears hopefully one of them—all of them preferably behind lock and key.

"No, me neither," I admitted.

"Circuses really aren't that popular anymore, are they?"

"No, I guess people nowadays favor other forms of entertainment," I said.

"Such a pity," he said. "Circuses are a lot of fun. With the trapeze artists and the clowns, and all the wild animals."

We'd now arrived at the spot where the cages containing these wild animals were located, and as we walked past them, I felt pity for the poor creatures. "Lions really shouldn't spend their time traveling around in circuses, though," I said. "They probably would be much happier in their natural habitat."

A particularly sleepy-looking lion now stared back at us from his cage, and opened his mouth to yawn.

"Hi, there," I said. "My name is Max and this is Dooley. Could we perhaps have a moment of your time, good sir?"

"Sure," said the lion. "What do you want?"

"Well, we're actually looking for one of our humans who's gone missing."

The lion laughed at this. "You misplaced your human, huh? Now there's something you don't hear every day."

"Yeah, he's gone and got himself kidnapped," I said. "So now we're trying to find him."

"And what does this human of yours look like may I ask?"

"Oh, he's big and a little heavyset, with a paunch and not much hair on top of his head."

"You've just described pretty much every single male over fifty that walks around this place all day," said the lion. "So I'm afraid you're gonna have to be more specific, cat."

"Max," I said. "The name is Max."

"Uncle Alec is a cop," Dooley specified. "He's chief of police and is usually dressed in his police uniform, complete with a holster where he likes to keep his gun safely tucked away, and his badge on his chest, and a cap on his head, and he drives a police car, too."

The lion smiled. "I'm afraid I haven't seen him, fellas. But maybe ask Bella over there. She gets around more than I do." He gestured to an elephant who was getting a nice scrub from one of her carers.

"Thanks, Mr. Lion," I said.

"Leo," the lion said. "And I hope you find your human. I wouldn't like losing my own human, to be honest."

I gave the lion a look of concern. "Do they–do they treat you well here, Leo?"

"Oh, sure," said Leo. "Can't complain. Plenty of food and plenty of exercise if that's what you mean. And the people taking care of me are nice enough. And if I promise not to chomp their heads off when they stick it between my teeth I get an extra snack in the evening, so life is pretty sweet as far as I'm concerned."

I gulped a little. I wouldn't want to be the person sticking my head between this big lion's teeth, but then humans are a little weird, as I think I've reiterated more than once.

"I wonder what life must be like for a lion like Leo," said

Dooley as we walked on. "To have to do all kinds of tricks for food, I mean."

"Yeah, I wouldn't want to be in his place," I said.

"Though in a sense Odelia expects us to perform tricks in exchange for food, too, right?"

I hadn't looked at it that way, but Dooley was right. We were playing detective in exchange for board and lodging. "I guess so," I said therefore. "Though at least she doesn't lock us up in a cage."

We'd arrived at Bella's dwelling, and I recognized her from the parade we'd seen the day we spent in the company of Charlene.

"Hi, Bella!" I said, raising my voice a little, as Bella was towering over us. She was an impressive animal, and now sat in a large tub, her back being scrubbed with a big brush.

Bella looked down at us with a curious look. "Hi, cats," she said finally.

"Leo told us you might be able to help us," said Dooley. "Our human has gone missing. He's a police chief who wears a police chief's uniform, a police chief's cap and drives a police chief's car. He's also very large and has no hair on his head. So have you seen him maybe, Miss Bella?"

The elephant laughed. "I'm sorry, you guys, but I don't think I've seen anyone answering to that description, I'm afraid."

"Oh," said Dooley, visibly disappointed.

"The thing is, strange things have been happening, Miss Bella," I said. "People have been going to see Madame Solange and their wishes have all been granted, but then it turns out it's all bogus. Fake lottery tickets, stolen items, and cases of outright fraud. And it all started when the fair set up in Hampton Cove. So now we're thinking there might be a connection."

"Oh, and our human doesn't remember us," said Dooley, deciding to reveal all to this elephant.

"Sounds like you guys are in a real pickle," said Bella. "Lucky for me my human hasn't forgotten me yet. For if he did, there would be hell to pay." And to show us what she meant, she lightly patted her carer on the head.

I gulped, thinking I wouldn't want to risk the wrath of this particular elephant. "So you can't help us, then?" I asked.

"I'm afraid not, cat," said Bella, "though if you want to talk about strange happenings taking place, I can absolutely relate. For one thing, the circus director disappeared a few months back, only to suddenly turn up again a couple of days ago. So go figure."

"And who's the director of the circus?" I asked, though of course I already knew this.

"Solange's husband. Guy called Wolf Moonblood," said the elephant. "Solange was really sad when he disappeared, and she's been very happy since his triumphant return, so at least that story has a happy ending." She smiled down at us. "I hope your story will have a happy ending, too." And to show us she had her big heart in the right place, she suddenly showered us with a spray of soapy water.

So we quickly skedaddled, but not before trying to shake off this impromptu shower!

When Odelia walked into Madame Solange's lair for the second time in two days, she didn't exactly know what to expect. At the very least she wanted to dig a little deeper into the mystery of her mom losing part of her memory the day before, after their joint consultation.

As she walked in, the guard gave her the same unfriendly glare he'd awarded her the day before, and she saw that a sign had been hung up in the waiting room, a disclosure that the consults were being filmed and if you didn't want your consult to be filmed you had to tell Madame Solange before the session began.

Moments later the curtain shifted and the fortune teller beckoned her in.

"Back again, huh?" said Solange with a smile. "Couldn't get enough of my predictions?"

"Not exactly," said Odelia as she took a seat, and watched how Solange removed the doily from her crystal ball. "Look, something happened to my mom after we came to see you yesterday. She's been acting very strange."

"Strange, how?"

"Well, she doesn't remember my boyfriend, for one thing, and now she insists he goes out on a date with you instead."

Solange grinned at this. "I'm sorry, hon, but I'm a happily married woman, so..." Then she turned serious. "Has she suffered memory loss before?"

"No, but I lost track of her yesterday for a while, and when we finally found her she was wandering around in the fields near here, barefoot and obviously confused. She also doesn't remember what happened."

"So maybe she took a stumble and hit her head?" Solange shrugged. "I don't think you can hold me responsible, Miss..."

"Poole," said Odelia. "Odelia Poole. And I'm not holding you responsible, but lots of strange things have been happening since you set up shop in my town, so..."

"So now you're blaming me for... what exactly?" asked Solange, her smile having been replaced by a slight look of annoyance.

"I'm not blaming you for anything. Just saying it's an awfully strange coincidence, that's all."

Both women faced off for a moment, then the fortune teller said, "Fine. Wait here a moment, will you? I think I might be able to help you." And abruptly she took off through another curtain and into a part of the trailer Odelia assumed were her private quarters. She heard Solange talking on the phone, and moments later the curtains through which Odelia had entered moved and a woman walked in. She looked a little like Solange, but was older and her face sported a hard look.

"Hi, I'm Solange's sister Selena," said the woman. "She told me you have some kind of complaint?"

"I have no complaint," said Odelia as Solange joined them and now both women stared down at her, none too friendly.

Suddenly she didn't feel entirely safe anymore, and wished she hadn't come.

Selena took a seat on Solange's chair and said, "Now look here, Miss Poole..."

"Yes?" said Odelia, and made the mistake of looking straight into the woman's eyes. They were a very dark green, she saw. And all of a sudden she was feeling a little weak. And before long a sense of nausea and dizziness started washing over her.

She was vaguely aware that the woman was talking to her, though for the life of her she couldn't tell what she was saying.

And then the floor was racing up to her and darkness closed in from all sides...

❧

*D*ooley and I were more or less aimlessly wandering around the fairground. Our interviews with the animals making up the wild animal contingent of Circus Moonblood hadn't exactly given us much to go on—if anything. And since we didn't want to set paw inside Madame Solange's trailer again, we decided to take a look around, hoping to stumble upon the kind of clue leading to the unraveling of this deepening mystery.

"Do you think Marge will get her memory back, Max?" asked Dooley.

"I hope so. It wouldn't be nice if she didn't."

"She can't even talk to us anymore. Which is really strange, don't you think?"

"Yeah, I do."

"What if Odelia also loses her memory? Or Gran? Then none of our humans would be able to talk to us."

"That wouldn't be good," I agreed. "Though the chance of

Odelia forgetting who we are is very slim, Dooley. Non-existent, even."

Just then, I suddenly thought I saw Odelia being ushered out of Madame Solange's trailer, and so we both quickly made our way over to report—though really there wasn't all that much to say.

"Odelia!" I said as we trailed after her. She was acting a little strange, I thought, not at all steady on her feet and staggering around like a drunken sailor.

She was leaning against another trailer, this one announcing it sold the most delicious caramel apples in the Western hemisphere, and the moment we caught up with her, Dooley happily said, "So did you get your fortune told, Odelia?"

Odelia stared at us for a moment, then said, "Oh, hi, cats. I like cats," she announced, then promptly threw up right then and there!

"Looks like she ate a bad caramel apple," Dooley said.

"So we talked to the lion and the elephant," I said, "and they both say they haven't seen Uncle Alec. They're also not aware that anything out of the ordinary is going on."

"I gotta get out of here," Odelia muttered, wiping her lips. "Bye, cats."

"Bye, Odelia," I said, confused. Then, on a hunch, I added, "You can still understand us though, can't you?"

But instead of responding, she just walked off!

So I quickly followed her and said, "Odelia? Talk to us, please?"

But she continued to simply ignore us!

"Odelia?" I said, concern making me a little anxious. "Is everything all right?"

Then, suddenly, she said, "What's with all the meowing, cat? Can't you see I have no food for you? Now get lost. Go back to your owner—if you have an owner."

And with these words, she stumbled off.

Dooley and I shared a look of shock.

"She forgot about us, Max!" said Dooley, summing up the state of affairs very succinctly. "She's completely forgotten that we exist!"

43

*C*hase was starting to feel like an automaton after having shown the picture of that boxer type fellow to anyone he saw. All of the people working at the fair gave him the same reply: 'Never seen the guy before, Detective.'

They did it with a certain shifty-eyed cautiousness that made him think that they knew perfectly well who the guy was but were either too intimidated to tell him the truth or were simply circling the wagons and giving this nosy cop the runaround.

And he'd just walked away from an awkward encounter with a juggler who gave him a very unfriendly stare in response to his question when suddenly he found himself coming face to face with... Chief Alec!

"Chief!" he cried, surprise making him a little squeaky-voiced. "Hey, there, buddy!"

But Alec wasn't responding with the same joyful surprise at this happy reunion. On the contrary, he simply stared at Chase as if he were a bug he'd just discovered in his potato salad. He didn't look like the Alec he knew, either: he was sporting some sort of ridiculous outfit: black leather jacket

211

and black leather pants, and on top of his head was a wig of some kind and his face had been festooned with sideburns and a mustache.

"Do I know you?" asked the Chief coldly.

"Alec, it's me—Chase!" he said, patting his own chest, then holding out a welcoming hand, which the other pointedly ignored.

"I'm afraid you must be mistaking me with someone else," said Alec. "My name is Wolf Moonblood, not... what did you call me?"

"Alec Lip," said Chase, sobered to some extent. He was pretty sure he wasn't mistaken, so he approached the guy and grabbed his ridiculous hair and yanked it off.

As he'd surmised, it was just a wig.

"Hey!" said Alec, grabbing at his now hairless head. "What do you think you're doing!"

"What's going on, Alec?" asked Chase. "Don't you remember me?"

"Give me back my hair," said Alec coldly.

Chase frowned, then decided to take things a little further still, and took a good grip on the man's mustache and gave it a yank. It easily came off, and now he was holding both the man's hair and his mustache. Only those ridiculous sideburns were left.

"Hey! This is assault!" said the Chief. "I'll have your badge for this, you ridiculous..."

"Alec, buddy!" said Chase. "I don't know what's gotten into you, but you gotta snap out of it!" And for good measure he snapped his fingers in the man's face a couple times.

Alec blinked, then frowned. "I would like to have my hair and mustache back now."

"Oh, for crying out loud!" said Chase, and took a firm grip on the man's sideburns and pulled. There was a slight ripping sound, and both came off in his hands, too!

And there he stood: Chief Alec Lip, large as life, and looking decidedly dazed after having been divested of all of his facial hair.

But before Chase could slap the man on the back and invite him for a drink to tell him what had happened, suddenly three burly men arrived on the scene and attached themselves to his arms and started to drag him off instead!

"Let go of me!" he bellowed, and fought them off as well as he could. Now Chase was a powerfully built man, but he was no match for three brutes like this, and before long he was being muscled off the premises and deposited squarely at the entrance to the fair.

"And stay away!" warned the biggest and toughest of the trio.

"I'm a cop!" he said, and showed them his badge. "And you're holding a man prisoner!"

"Oh, buzz off, cop," said one of the goons with a shrug.

"I'll be back," he warned.

"Promises, promises," said the guy, who had a cleanly shaven head, was wearing red Converse shoes, had a crooked nose, cauliflower ears, a tattoo of a skull and crossbones on his neck and spoke with a Boston accent. And only then Chase realized that *this* man resembled *that* man very closely indeed—the man he was looking for!

He now took the picture he'd been showing around out of his pocket.

"This is you," he said.

The man glanced at the picture, then at Chase, and said, "No, it's not."

"Yeah, it is!"

The man looked over to his musclebound colleagues, and they must have exchanged some sort of secret silent code, for moments later they had attached themselves to Chase's arms again, and this time proceeded to drag him in the opposite direction!

"Hey, you can't do this to me!" said Chase.

"Oh, shut up already," grunted Cauliflower Ear. "Why is it you people always have to come and ruin things for us."

"Heeeeelp!" Chase yelled, feeling a little annoyed he had to ask for help from others while he was usually so capable of taking care of himself. "I'm being abducted!"

But then Cauliflower Ear grunted something, hauled off, and planted a meaty fist on Chase's jaw, and all of a sudden the lights went out and the world turned dark.

*O*fficer Sarah Flunk was feeling a little blue. Her boyfriend of several months had finally proposed, only for him to tell Detective Kingsley he'd only proposed after being coerced, which made the whole thing leave a very sour taste in the young police officer's mouth. In fact she wouldn't mind smacking Barry in the face right now, the bastard.

And as she showed the picture of that unsavory character who'd forced Barry into proposing marriage to her while also having a hand in Chief Alec's kidnapping to another stallkeeper, she suddenly became aware of a fracas or altercation (or even a skirmish), so she heaved a deep sigh and headed on over to see what was going on.

Great was her surprise when she found none other than her commanding officer Detective Kingsley staggering around, looking as if he'd drunk more than he was used to.

"Detective Kingsley, sir," she said while bystanders laughed at the drunk cop. "Let's get you out of here." And she started leading the inebriated cop away from the scene.

He was leaning heavily on her, which was a little inconvenient as he was almost twice her size, but she still managed to put some distance between themselves and the onlookers. "What happened, sir?" she asked once they were on their way to the parking lot.

"Who are you?" asked Chase, a distinct slur to his speech.

"What do you mean?" Oh, God, he was completely off his face, wasn't he?

"What do you mean what do I mean? Who are you and who am I?"

"I'm Sarah, sir. Sarah Flunk? And you're Chase Kingsley. Detective Chase Kingsley with the Hampton Cove Police Department."

"Who?"

"How much did you have to drink, sir?" she said, shocked at his behavior. Chase usually was so well-behaved, and a stickler for protocol and correct procedure, too.

"Where am I?" the cop asked now.

"At the fair," said Sarah in clipped tones. She really liked Chase, both as a colleague and a human being, but there were limits to what she could tolerate from anyone, and she drew the line at public drunkenness, and certainly drinking on duty. "We're looking for Chief Alec, remember?"

"Who's Chief Alec?" slurred Chase, his eyes swiveling in every direction.

Just then, Sarah saw Odelia Poole. "Odelia!" she called out. "Can you please help me put Chase in a car? He's completely wasted."

Odelia gave her a strange look, then said, "Who are you and what are you talking about?"

"Your boyfriend is drunk!" said Sarah emphatically. She didn't like to be put in this situation.

Odelia looked at her, then looked at Chase, then said, "I've never seen this man before in my life. Now leave me alone!"

4 4

*T*o say that we were feeling a little under the weather was an understatement. First one of our humans had lost her mind, and now the second one! If this kept up, Dooley's fear that all three of the humans who could talk to us would soon be lost to us was going to become a reality!

"It's this Madame Solange, Max!" said Dooley. "She must have done something to Odelia—she simply must have!"

"I think you're right, Dooley," I said. "But how do we prove it?"

We'd taken up position not far from Solange's trailer, trying to figure out how to proceed. So far we hadn't come up with a single plan, the emotion of seeing our favorite human in the world looking at us like a dead fish having completely discombobulated us.

Just then, Norm came buzzing over. "Have I got news for you guys!" said the spy fly.

"And we've got some news for you," I said. "Odelia has suddenly developed an acute case of memory loss and now she doesn't even know who we are!"

"Or is able to understand a word we say!" Dooley added, looking distinctly down in the dumps, as did I, for that matter.

"I think I know what's going on here, fellas!" said Norm. "I was in there just now, when Odelia was being hypnotized!"

"Hypnotized?" I asked, staring at the fearless fly.

"Hypnotized!" he repeated. "Apparently Solange didn't like the questions Odelia was asking, so she called her sister, who came over immediately, and proceeded to put some kind of spell on her. Odelia blacked out, and when she came to, they kicked her out!"

"But... how is that even possible!"

"Oh, it's possible," said Norm. "I saw them do it, and while Odelia was under, they were saying how she wouldn't remember a thing—not who Solange was, or why she was there—or even her own name!"

"So that's how they do it," I said. "Hypnosis!"

"I've seen a documentary on hypnosis," said Dooley, "on the Discovery Channel. It's not very nice. They can make people do almost anything. In the documentary they made a man eat worms, after convincing him it wasn't worms but potato chips. He thought it was delicious but it looked really, really gross!"

Norm stared at Dooley for a moment, then shook his head. "No, they didn't feed Odelia worms. But they did convince her to forget anything to do with the fair, or Solange or the investigation."

"Oh, this is so not good," I said. "Now she'll never be the same again."

"They can be cured, though," said Dooley. "There is some kind of code word they use and when they say it, the person snaps out of it." He smiled. "You should have seen the look on the man's face when he realized he'd eaten a whole plate full of worms!"

"Nice, Dooley," I said, though I was relieved to hear that Odelia could be cured, and so could Marge, who probably had been the victim of the same tactic.

"Oh, and they just did the same thing to Chase," said Norm. "A couple of really big guys brought him in, completely unconscious, and this sister of Madame Solange, whose name is Selena, by the way, revived him, and then, while they held him down, did the same thing to him she did to Odelia. So I'm afraid now you have two humans who won't even remember their own names, you guys."

"Oh, God," I said. I darted a glance at the trailer of this Solange person, and wondered how we were going to stop her from hypnotizing the entire town of Hampton Cove! Just then, a man hoisting a camera on his shoulder, and another man holding a microphone, downed tools right next to where we were hiding under the trailer. They shook a couple of cigarettes out of a packet and lit them, then took a long drag.

"I hate this job," confessed the cameraman. "When is it going to be finished?"

"Not until the brass figure we've got enough footage," said the microphone guy.

"And when will that be? I reckon we've got plenty of footage already." He ticked it off on his nicotine-stained fingers. "We've got hours and hours of Solange doing her trick, dozens of clients on tape, and we've interviewed the entire staff of this stupid circus and everyone else involved. The only ones we haven't talked to are the animals!"

"Look, we just gotta keep on going," said his colleague. "We sure get paid enough."

"You think? Peanuts, man, compared to what Solange and her family are netting."

"You know something I don't?"

"A hundred and fifty million bucks!"

Microphone Man whistled through his teeth. "Woo-wee. That's a lot of dough."

"You bet it is. Hotflix is clearly betting on a runaway hit, and I'll bet they'll get it, too."

"Another Kardashians, only this time with a slightly more unusual family."

"Keeping up with the Moonbloods," said Camera Guy with a grin, then took another long drag from his cancer stick and dumped the butt right next to Dooley and me, stubbing it out with his foot.

"There's been talk of the miracles all being bogus, though," said his colleague. "Cops are getting involved."

"Yeah, I heard that, too. But who cares, right? It's just a show. And as long as the ratings go through the roof, Solange and company will keep raking in the millions."

And then he dumped his cigarette butt, too, and both men were off.

We watched them enter Solange's trailer, presumably to film some more footage of unsuspecting Hampton Covians being promised the moon by Solange and her sister.

Before Dooley and I could discuss what we'd just discovered, a man suddenly came hurrying in the direction of the trailer. It was Wolf Moonblood—only he had a wig haphazardly placed on top of his head, sideburns equally haphazardly pasted to his cheeks, and his mustache was completely askance.

He entered the trailer, crying, "Solange! Solange! Some guy messed up my hair!"

Dooley and I shared a look of understanding.

"Dooley," I said. "I think we just cracked this case."

"And me!" said Norm excitedly. "I cracked it, too, right?"

"You did the heavy lifting, Norm," I said with a smile.

And for a tiny fly that was a real feat.

*G*ran was reluctantly ambling along, taking in the sights and sounds of the fair that had graced her town with its presence. Next to her, Scarlett was teetering along on her high heels, and alternately nibbling and sucking at an ice cream cone.

"You have to lick it," said Vesta, watching the spectacle with distaste.

"What are you talking about?" asked her friend, smacking her lips.

"You lick ice cream, not bite it or suck it—you lick it. With your tongue."

"Look, it's my ice cream so I'll do what I want with it." Scarlett attacked the thing again, making horrible sucking sounds as she did. "If you don't like it, get your own."

"I hate fairs," Vesta grumbled.

"That's because you hate everything."

"No, I don't. I like TV. And I like…" She paused, trying to think of what else she liked, until she caught Scarlett's grin and grunted, "Oh, shut up."

"I didn't say anything!"

"But you were thinking it!"

"Oh, so now I can't even think what I want?"

"You know what I mean." Her granddaughter had convinced her to tag along while a big police operation was being conducted to find Vesta's missing son. She didn't have high hopes. The cops in this town didn't exactly have a great track record catching the bad guys. Instead they kept arresting Vesta and Scarlett, even when they hadn't done anything wrong!

So when she caught sight of a couple of officers sticking a piece of paper with a mug shot of the suspect under people's noses, she sniffed annoyedly.

"What? You don't think they'll find your son?" asked Scarlett.

"They couldn't find my son if he danced in front of them dressed in nothing but a hula skirt," she said. She frowned as she suddenly saw Sarah Flunk escorting Chase off the scene, the latter looking a little ill-footed for some reason. "Will you look at that? I think Chase just went and got himself in trouble."

"I like Chase. I think he's a great cop, and he's not bad-looking either," said Scarlett.

"Watch it, you," said Vesta, wagging a bony finger in her friend's face.

"What did I say this time?!"

"Chase is spoken for, you know that."

"I just said—"

"I know what you said, and I know how your mind works, and you're not going to—holy cow, what's going on over there?"

She'd suddenly spotted her cats, waving frantically at her from underneath a trailer.

She hurriedly joined them, as did Scarlett, though at a slower pace, due to those damn high heels she always insisted on wearing.

"What's wrong?" she asked once she'd crouched down, her knees creaking as she did.

"It's Odelia," said Max. "She's been hypnotized."

"And Chase, too!" said Dooley.

"And so has Uncle Alec!" Max added.

"And he's lost his hair and his mustache and his sideburns!"

"And can you even understand what we're saying or have they gotten to you too?!"

She stared down at her cats. "I can understand you loud and clear," she said. "And what's all this stuff about hypnotizing?"

"Who's been hypnotized?" asked Scarlett.

"Will you please be quiet? I'm trying to talk to my cats."

"In any other universe that sentence would earn you a one-way trip to the nuthouse," Scarlett announced.

"Madame Solange has a sister," said Max. "And that sister has been going around hypnotizing people, and making them forget who they are. She hypnotized Odelia just now, and Chase, too, and probably also Marge and Uncle Alec."

"And now Uncle Alec thinks he's a man named Wolf and he's married to Solange!" Dooley finished.

"What are they saying?" asked Scarlett.

"Can you just be quiet for two seconds?"

"We also overheard two men talking," Max continued, darting anxious glances around, "and the family of Solange has signed a contract with Hotflix for one hundred and fifty million dollars for an exclusive reality show. Which is going to show how she makes people's every wish come true. Like a modern-day Santa Claus, only the female version. And so Solange and her family have been going around making sure those wishes all come true—only they haven't. Not really. They've been faking the whole thing. But the network doesn't care. As long as the ratings go through the roof, they just don't care."

"Oh, my God," said Vesta, getting up and rubbing her painful knees. She turned to her friend. "Bad business, honey. Very bad."

But Scarlett was looking the other way, her arms crossed in front of her chest and pointedly ignoring her.

"Now what?" asked Vesta.

"Do I have permission to speak, General? Are you absolutely sure, Your Highness?"

"Yeah, you have permission to speak."

"Well, now I don't wanna—so there."

"Solange's sister has been going around hypnotizing people to forget they exist."

"Who exists?"

"They! Solange and her family! And they've been making people's wishes come true for this big reality show they're doing—a contract worth nine figures if you please!"

"Nine figures!"

Vesta nodded. "So how do we handle this is what I want to know. This Solange is clearly a very dangerous woman, and her sister even more so."

Scarlett then slowly turned to her, a smile forming on her lips, and Vesta could just see the thought forming in her friend's head, and the same smile soon spread across her own features.

"The watch is on this, buddy," said Scarlett, holding out her hand.

"Yeah, we got this," Vesta confirmed, and tickled Scarlett's fingers with her own. She then looked down at Max and Dooley, and the fly that kept buzzing around their heads. "I've got a very important assignment for you guys. Are you game?"

"Just don't forget about us, Gran," said Dooley. "Please don't forget who we are!"

"Oh, I can promise you that I won't, Dooley," she said.

"That's what Odelia said," said the small gray cat sadly. "And look what happened to her."

&.

Solange had just promised a middle-aged woman that any day now she'd come into the possession of a very large sum of money when suddenly the curtain of her domain was thrown wide and a very irate-looking Ida Baumgartner came charging in, a smallish man in tow.

"You promised me my husband would return to me!" Ida bellowed. "And look what I found on my doorstep this morning. This weird-looking creature!"

"My name is Burt Baumgartner," the small guy intoned. "And I have returned from the dead to love my wife for all eternity!"

"This is not my husband!" said Ida. "This is Barney Grogan—the butcher!"

"I love you, Ida," said the little guy, and puckered up his lips for a kiss, earning himself a ringing smack around the head from Ida.

"He doesn't even look like my husband!" Ida cried.

"I'm very sorry," said Solange, throwing an apologetic glance at her other client, who stood watching the scene with interest. "For customer complaints I'll have to refer you to my sister. She's over in the next trailer. She'll happily assist you in this matter."

"I will always love you, Ida, dear," said the smallish man, adjusting his glasses.

"Oh, go away, Barney," said Ida, and both of them walked out.

Solange rolled her eyes. Clearly her sister was starting to miss the ball lately. First this whole business with Wolf's family, and now this? If she kept this up even Hotflix would start doubting the fat check they'd written them.

The client left her trailer, after Solange once more promised her that the money would arrive any day now, and she quickly glanced into the waiting area, and saw she had no more customers. Great. She needed a break.

But before she could withdraw into her private lair, suddenly the sound of a cat mewling made itself heard right outside the trailer door.

"Oh, for crying out loud!" she said, and stalked over. "How many times do I have to tell you not to let—" But the man she'd been scolding for gross negligence wasn't standing sentry as he usually was. "Maxim?!" she called out. Where the hell was that no-good lazy bum now? So she opened the door to take a look, and suddenly felt a jolt like she'd never felt before. It was as if she'd been struck by lightning. And then she was going down, her face hitting the ground before she knew what had hit her.

And just before she passed out, she thought she caught a glimpse of a little old lady with white hair, holding a very big Taser in her hand, and giving her a big toothy grin.

EPILOGUE

I lazily opened one eye to take in the scene. Odelia was there, of course, and so was Chase. In fact our human's entire family was there: Tex and Marge, Uncle Alec and Charlene, and Gran and Scarlett.

All of them were seated around the garden table, with Chase expertly flipping burgers and making sure his (future) family members were all taken care of—food-wise.

Marge and Odelia had had their memories returned to them, and so had Uncle Alec, though the latter still had a tendency from time to time to touch his hair, presumably hoping to find it thick and lush and gelled in place. What he found instead were the few stray wispy strings that had been there for a while—much to his disappointment, too. I didn't doubt that at some point in the future he'd order himself a nice toupee or wig.

Chase, too, had had his memory restored, and now remembered who he was and where he was and how he'd gotten there. And our humans could talk to us again, imagine that!

It had taken some arm-twisting on Gran's part to make

that miracle happen, but Solange's sister Selena had finally agreed to reverse the spell she'd put on the Poole family members, and they'd soon snapped out of their hypnotism-induced funk.

Charlene, too, had been saved from the kind of feverish spell she'd been under, and it was safe to say things had mostly returned to normal. In her case it had been a little trickier, as Selena had hypnotized her over one of her goons' phones. As a consequence the spell had taken longer to take hold, but was more pernicious, and harder to reverse.

"So all this for a little bit of money?" asked Harriet.

"Not a little bit," I said. "Unless you think one hundred and fifty million is nothing."

"It is a lot," she allowed, "but they never would have gotten away with it, would they?"

"I think they might have," I said. "If they could have just kept on hypnotizing people and sending their goons around to make people's wishes come true." Like Santa's elves, if Santa's elves had joined the Mob.

"Amazing," said Brutus, but he was referring to the piece of delicious turkey meat Odelia had handed us, not the case of Solange and Selena.

"I still think it's a sad story," said Dooley. "Solange must really have missed her husband to go to such lengths."

"Yeah, but she shouldn't have kidnapped Uncle Alec just because she missed her husband," I said.

As it happened, Solange's husband Wolf had died six months before, breaking his neck when he fell from the roof of his circus tent. And because he had no insurance, Solange and her sister decided not to tell anyone he'd died. They simply buried the body in the town where Circus Moonblood had been set up at the time, and pretended he'd skedaddled after a fight with his wife. She'd missed her husband, of course, and so had the circus, which had to go on without its leader. There had been some grumblings in the ranks about the leadership the sisters were extending, and it became clear they needed a new boss to firmly take the reins. And then one day Uncle Alec and Charlene dropped by Madame Solange for a session. Solange had immediately noticed the resemblance to her late husband, and so she and her sister decided on a wild scheme: they'd abducted the Chief, dressed him up as Wolf, and with some of Selena's hypnotic trickery, Chief Alec had actually believed he was Wolf Moonblood and so had everyone else!

"Do you remember anything?" asked Scarlett now. "Anything at all?"

The Chief gave her a rueful look. "Not much. I do remember I had to feed the elephant one day and he must have smelled that I wasn't Wolf for he gave me a really weird look and then smacked me in the face with his trunk!"

They all laughed at that, but I thought it was pretty smart of Bella. At least she hadn't been hoodwinked the way the others had. Of course if Dooley and I had managed to get up close and personal with 'Wolf' I'm pretty sure we would have known he was in fact Chef Alec, too.

I placed my head on my paws again. I'd eaten my fill and now it was time for a nap.

"Chase is a much better grill master than Tex," said Dooley, chewing delightedly.

"Yeah, he certainly is," I muttered sleepily.

"I thought he and Tex were taking a barbecue cooking class?" asked Brutus.

"Oh, they did," said Harriet. "But Tex set fire to the kitchen on his first day, so they banned him from the class."

"Too bad," said Dooley. "I think Tex really likes to grill— only he has zero talent."

"Just like I love to act, but I have zero talent, too," I mumbled.

"So is Hotflix going to air the new show?" asked Brutus.

"Nope," said Harriet. "And WLBC-9 have cut all ties with them after the whole fiasco."

Hotflix had struck a deal with the network, filming the whole thing under the local station's banner and pretending they were creating a documentary, not wanting the new show to be announced before it was in the can. But the two companies had fallen out after Solange and Selena had been arrested. Now only the lawyers would benefit.

"Do you think I should grow a mustache, though?" asked Uncle Alec, thoughtfully rubbing his upper lip.

"No, I don't," said Charlene crisply, and promptly slapped his hand away.

The Mayor still hadn't completely forgiven her boyfriend for spending time in another woman's bed—even though he claimed to have no recollection whatsoever.

"Burger up!" Chase yelled, and loud cheers rang out all around the table.

The sun was shining, birds were tweeting, our humans were happily prattling, meat was sizzling on the grill, spreading its delicious aroma, and all in all I thought all was well with the world. And I would have dozed off, if Norm hadn't suddenly buzzed up to me, and announced happily, "Max! Buddy!"

I opened my eyes and heaved a deep sigh. "Norm, hi," I said. We hadn't seen the big fly around for a while. "How are things in the world of the flies?"

"Oh, great!" said the indomitable spy fly. "You remember how you told me I'd always have a home in your home?"

"Of course," I said. "As long as you don't touch my food you can buzz around as much as you want." I'd even told Odelia as much, and she'd specifically instructed her family members not to take out the fly swatter if they saw Norm buzzing about.

"So do you remember you also told me I could bring along my family if I wanted to?" Norm now asked, still buzzing in front of my nose.

"Uh-huh," I said.

"Oh, Max, you didn't," said Harriet.

"Oh, yes, I did," I said. "Norm has done so much for this family that it's only right for us to give something back."

"But, Max—"

"It's done, Harriet."

"But, Max!"

I held up my paw, to indicate that as far as I was concerned, the discussion was over. She closed her lips with a click of the teeth, and proceeded to give me a furious look. I know I probably should have discussed this with my house-mates, but it was the right thing to do!

"Thank you so much, Max," said Norm, buzzing up and down with obvious glee. "So I've brought my family over, and they're all anxious to meet my benefactor, the great M."

"Oh, that's sweet," I said with a tired smile. This case had taken a lot out of me, and I frankly needed to catch up on my sleep. Then again, I didn't want to be rude, and so I was more than willing to say hi to Norm's mom and dad, and his siblings, too.

"Come on over, you guys!" Norm yelled. "Meet my best friend Max!"

But before Norm's family could join us for this happy occasion, suddenly a large cloud blocked out the sun. It was so large that the entire backyard was plunged into darkness, and the Pooles all glanced up in surprise.

"What's going on?" asked Charlene.

"I didn't know it was going to rain," said Uncle Alec, holding out his hand.

"'Sunny,' it says here," said Marge, referring to the weather app on her phone.

"It's because you didn't let me near the grill," said Tex moodily. "Nature is feeling my mood."

"We didn't let you near the grill, honey," said Marge, "because we don't enjoy being poisoned on a weekly basis."

"Now you're just being mean."

"I still love you, though," said his wife, and planted a kiss on the sulking doctor's cheek.

"It's not a cloud," said Gran suddenly. "It's…"

"Flies!" Scarlett yelled. "And I'm wearing my brand-new white dress!"

She was right. Before our very eyes, hundreds of flies suddenly came buzzing over to where we were pleasantly lounging on the porch swing. Did I say hundreds? I meant thousands—maybe even millions!

They were suddenly everywhere: on our fur, on the table, on the potato salad, the coleslaw, the baby carrots, on the nice sausages, the steaks, the ribs, the burgers, swarming around our humans, and generally acting like an invasion army!

"Heeeeelp!" said Scarlett, swatting them away. "They're in my hair!"

They were in everyone's hair!

"Well, Max!" said Norm, over the deafening droning noise of the swarming insects. "Now these are my brothers and sisters—and my aunts and uncles—and my cousins and my nieces and nephews… on my mother's side. My dad's side got held up when a farmer dumped a truckload of manure on his cornfield and they couldn't resist a free buffet so they'll get here a little bit later. Guys, this is Max! Or M as I like to call him!"

"Norm—how many are there!" I yelled, afraid to open my mouth for fear they'd simply swarm in and start buzzing around inside my tummy!

"Oh, I don't know," he said with a smile. "I have a big

family, but then that's flies for you—we love our crazy, big fly families."

I glanced over and saw that Harriet was eyeing me furiously. "Flies breed like... flies, Max, didn't you know? There are probably millions! And now they'll all come and live with us. In our house! Eating our food! And... defecating all over the place!"

Oh, dear. I'd really gone and done it this time, hadn't I?

"It's all right, Max," said Dooley, though it was hard to make out his features through the haze of flies. "You did it out of kindness, and the universe rewards acts of kindness."

Our humans were frantically clearing the table and escaping inside, and Harriet and Brutus were escaping in the direction of the bushes at the bottom of the garden, and soon it was just me and Dooley and Norm and his million-strong family.

"Ma!" Norm yelled. "Come over here and meet Max!"

A very large fly materialized out of the swarm and greeted me warmly. "Thanks for being such a good friend to my Norm, Max. He's a good boy, my Norm is. A little rambunctious, maybe, but he's got his heart in the right place. Now could you please tell him to find himself a nice girl and settle down—maybe he'll listen to you. He certainly doesn't listen to me, the little rascal!" And she proceeded to give her son a stern look. At least I think she did. It's kinda hard to read a fly's facial expressions, if you know what I mean.

"Oh, Mom. There's plenty of time for that sort of thing!" Norm said laughingly.

And as Dooley and I watched on, Norm's family attacked the food our humans had left on the table. I think it's safe to say this was not my finest hour, but at least, as Dooley had suggested, the universe would probably reward me for my kindness, right?

"Maybe we can ask Solange's sister to hypnotize them," said Dooley after a while. "Make them forget we exist, you know. She seems to be really good at that sort of thing."

I watched as Marge's nice white table cloth quickly turned a muddy brown.

And then we decided to flee the scene, too. So we hopped down from the swing and hurried inside through the pet flap. But who was I kidding? Flies are hard to keep out, and soon they were following us inside, buzzing around everywhere we looked.

Our humans were all seated around the kitchen table, and giving me hard looks.

"Max," said Gran suddenly. "This is your doing, isn't it?"

"Um…" I said, prevaricating mightily. But Gran's stare is something else, so quickly I hung my head. "Yeah, it is," I admitted. "I told Norm he could bring his family over—and he has."

"Oh, dear," said Marge, watching as her clean kitchen window was now speckled with hundreds of tiny dark spots.

But then Gran and Scarlett shared a look, and suddenly Gran brought out a stun gun, and Scarlett what looked like a can of mace. They both got up, and Gran bellowed, "Flies! You have ten seconds to leave this house or we'll zap you straight back to where you came from! We are the neighborhood watch, and we are not kidding around!"

Norm came buzzing up to me, looking a little nervous. "What's going on?" he asked.

"New assignment, Norm," I said, darting an anxious look at Gran and Scarlett, who were now counting down from ten to one. "Your mission, if you choose to accept it, is to head on over to the other side of town, and… and…"

"See what Bella and Leo are up to," Dooley added.

"Yeah," I said, giving Dooley a grateful smile. "And better take your family with you."

"My entire family?!" Norm said excitedly.

"Of course. If they're cut from the same cloth as you are, they'll prove invaluable to the service. Wonderful spies, one and all."

"Oh, Max—that's so generous of you! So what's the file on Bella and Leo?"

"Um… well, we've received credible intel that they might be foreign agents."

"We're on it, sir!" said Norm, and before Gran's countdown had ended, he and the rest of his family had all buzzed off.

"See!" Gran cried as she watched the swarm of flies all disappear. "The watch rules!"

We decided to let her enjoy her moment of triumph. After all, she had saved this family from certain doom, not to mention several family members of eternal memory loss. The watch might not be the success story Gran had envisioned when she started it, but it wasn't a total failure either.

"What are you going to do when Norm returns from his 'mission?'" asked Odelia as she gave us a cuddle. Contrary to her grandmother, she knew who'd saved the day.

"We'll just give him another one," I said with a smile.

She hugged us close, and we both hugged her right back. We'd almost lost our human to Solange's shenanigans, and it had made me realize just how lucky we were to have Odelia —and the rest of her family, too. There might not be millions of them, like Norm's impressive swarm, but when it comes to family I guess it's not about the quantity, but about the quality. And I can proudly say we had the best family any cat could hope for.

Suddenly Odelia stared at me with a frown. "I'm sorry," she said. "But do I know you?"

I looked up at her in alarm, and so did Dooley.

"Oh, no!" my friend said. "Max, it's happening again!"

But then Odelia's face broke into a wide grin. "Just kidding, you guys!"

Yep. The best human in the world.

And she's funny, too!

Or at least she thinks she is.

THE END

Thanks for reading! If you want to know when a new Nic Saint book comes out, sign up for Nic's mailing list: nicsaint.com/news.

EXCERPT FROM PURR
(THE MYSTERIES

Chapter One

There's a story someone once told me about not judging a person until you've walked a mile in their shoes. And I remember thinking at the time that this story doesn't really apply to cats, since we don't wear shoes. Still, the gist of the thing has always stuck with me, and when I now watched Odelia and Chase sweating and grunting their way through some sort of aerobics routine, I was reminded of this neat little aphorism or idiom.

It's hard for a cat to feel a lot of sympathy when humans put themselves through the wringer like this. I mean, no cat would willingly subject themselves to such silliness, but then that's humans for you. They must have some sort of masochistic streak, and like to torment themselves for no good reason whatsoever.

The shoes Odelia and Chase were wearing were sneakers, so I tried hard to picture myself wearing those same sneakers and jumping around like a crazy person, losing about a

eat in the process. Try as I might, though, I
uldn't see it.

hat are they doing?" asked Dooley, who'd been
erving the scene with the same stupefied expression on
his face as no doubt I was wearing on mine.

"It's called aerobics," I explained. "Humans do it to stay in
shape."

"What shape? Square or round or…"

"It doesn't matter as long as it's slim. Humans like to be
slim."

"It looks extremely painful," Dooley said, wincing a little
as Odelia practiced a high kick that looked very dangerous
indeed.

"Humans like to suffer," I explained.

"So weird," Dooley said with a shake of the head.

On the television a man was showing our humans how it
was done. He was a man with a big curly head of hair, a pink
sweat headband and very bright spandex clothes. Behind the
man were five women mimicking his every move, just the
way Odelia and Chase were, and the music pumping through
our living room speakers accompanying the man's instructions was loud and energetic. It also made my ears bleed.

Well, maybe not literally, but you know what I mean. Cats
have a very sensitive sense of hearing, and the noise from the
TV was very unpleasant to say the least.

I liked that Odelia wasn't alone, though. In case she pulled
a muscle, her boyfriend could immediately call for a doctor—
and she could do the same for him. Also, they say couples
who suffer together, stay together, and judging from the
pained grimaces on our humans' sweat-soaked faces, they
were suffering a lot, which boded well for their future.

"You would think that after spending so much time with
our humans we would understand what they're up to," said

Dooley. "But the opposite seems to be true. The longer I'm with them, the less I understand them."

"You certainly have a point, Dooley," I said, as I felt exactly the same way.

Suddenly the sliding glass door opened and Grandma Muffin walked in. She cast one look at her profusely sweating and grunting granddaughter and boyfriend, shook her head in dismay, and walked out again. Gran doesn't suffer fools gladly, and whatever she had to tell us could probably wait.

Suddenly the doorbell chimed, and since Odelia nor Chase reacted, I easily slid down from my perch on the couch and ambled over to see who it was.

Cats can't open doors, unfortunately, but they can take a peek through the letterbox and ascertain the identity of the person making a house call, which is what I did now.

Much to my surprise, the person standing in front of the door was the same person now working up a sweat on our television screen and shouting a good deal as he did.

For a moment I thought I was seeing things, for he looked exactly the same as he did on TV: that same curly head of hair, that same garishly colorful spandex outfit, and the same sneakers. Only the man at the door had a careworn expression on his face while the man on TV looked like he was about to reach his personal peak of pleasure.

So I padded into the living room again, and tried to attract Odelia's attention. It took me a while to accomplish this feat, as she was just demonstrating a very complicated routine that involved jumping up and down while waving her arms just so. Finally she dragged her eyes away from the screen and saw I was also waving my paws, only without defying gravity the way she was.

Immediately she turned down the sound. "Yes, Max?" she

said, panting heavily while planting her hands on her hips. "What do you want, buddy?"

"There's a man at the door," I said. "The same man that's on TV, in fact."

"Maybe he's here to give you some extra instructions," Dooley suggested.

"Yeah, that could be it," I said, nodding.

"He probably thinks you did something wrong and he wants to correct you in person," Dooley added as he placed his head on his front paws.

"What's going on?" asked Chase, who'd also become aware of this sudden lull in the proceedings.

Just then, the man at the door made his presence known once more by pressing his finger on the bell and this time keeping it here, causing it to jangle freely—usually a sure-fire way of making sure whoever is inside comes to the door post-haste.

Odelia now grabbed a towel and as she dabbed at her face hurried into the small hallway and opened the door. She must have been as surprised as I was to see her television fitness instructor in the flesh, for she stammered, "Mr. H-H-Hancock!"

"Odelia Poole?" asked the man, looking distinctly ill at ease. "The detective?"

"That's right—I mean, my name is Odelia Poole, but I'm not a detective. I'm a reporter, actually. With the Hampton Cove Gazette."

"I'm in trouble, Miss Poole. Big trouble. And I'm hoping you can help me."

"Yes—yes, of course," said Odelia, still visibly dazed by this strange coincidence.

When mere mortals meet their heroes in the flesh, they usually respond by turning both tongue-tied and weak-kneed, and I could observe this phenomenon up close and personal in my own human, who looked star-struck by this funny-looking fitness man.

"Can I come in?" asked Mr. Hancock after a moment in which Odelia did nothing more than goggle like a lovesick teenager meeting Justin Bieber for the first time.

"Yes! Yes, please do!" said Odelia, snapping out of her momentary stupor.

"Who is it, babe?" asked Chase as he came to see what was going on. When he caught sight of Mr. Hancock his jaw actually dropped and he just stood there, gawking.

Mr. Hancock smiled nervously, and since his onlookers were now both struck dumb, he did the honors himself by walking into our modest little home, closing the door. Then he said, "I only have four more days to live, Miss Poole, and I'm hoping you'll be able to find out who's doing this to me… and maybe stop them from murdering me."

Chapter Two

Harriet gazed before her into the middle distance, a worried look marring her usually smooth brow.

Next to her, Brutus glanced over, and when he caught the look of worry, reciprocated with a pang of concern himself. "The eyes?" he said.

Harriet nodded. "Yeah, I don't know what's happening, smoochie poo, but it looks like I don't see as well as I used to."

"Maybe we should tell someone?"

"No!" said Harriet immediately. "I don't want anyone to know. Promise me you won't tell a soul, Brutus. Not a single soul!"

"All right, all right," he said.

Harriet opened and closed one eye, then the other, but the object she was staring at didn't become any clearer. On the contrary, the rose bush on the other side of the backyard only seemed to become more blurred. Finally she shook her head in dismay. "I don't know what's happening, tootsie roll, but if this keeps up soon I won't be able to see a thing."

"I'm sure it's just temporary," said her partner, giving her a sweet little nudge.

Harriet's eyesight had been diminishing for the past couple of weeks now, and even though it wasn't something she liked to discuss with anyone—in fact only Brutus was aware of the baffling malady—it did give her great cause for concern.

Harriet prided herself in her twenty-twenty vision, like most cats do, and this sudden deterioration of what she'd always considered a natural ability was frankly worrying her to no slight degree.

"It could be our diet," she said now. "Maybe I'll ask Marge to put some more fresh meat in our diet. All that kibble and packaged food probably isn't very healthy."

"Yeah, good idea," said Brutus with a nod. "Or maybe Marge could feed us some of those vegetables humans like so much? Broccoli and, um, tomatoes?"

"Carrots!" said Harriet suddenly. "I've always heard carrots are good for the eyes, as they contain beta-carotene, so maybe I should start eating more carrots from now on."

"Uh-huh," said Brutus, though he clearly wasn't a big proponent of this theory.

"You know what? Maybe we can go on a diet together," she suggested now. "If I'm going to do this, it will be a big sacrifice, snickerdoodle. No more Cat Snax, and no more of those delicious wet food pouches. So let's do it together. It'll be much easier for me to keep up with my new dietary regimen if I have you right there doing it along with me."

Brutus gave her a startled look. "You mean... no more Cat Snax? No more... wet food?"

"That stuff isn't good for you anyway, sugar lump. And this way you'll join me on this health kick." She smiled as she gave her partner a loving nudge. "Thanks, snookums. I owe you one." And with these words, she disappeared inside to look for Marge and give her the good news.

A turtle was making its way through the undergrowth. She wasn't in a hurry, and when she came upon a fresh leaf that had recently fallen from an overhanging tree, she ate it at her leisure. It hadn't been long since she'd escaped her home, and this sojourn through the wide and open spaces was a real pleasure.

So when she came upon a black cat, muscular and built for action and speed, she eyed it with interest. Turtles, as a rule, are built for taking things slow and at their leisure, and coming upon this supreme specimen gave her a moment's pause, and even caused her to put down the tasty leaf so she could speak.

"Hi, there, sir," said the turtle. "Could you please tell me where I am? I seem to be lost."

The butch black cat glanced down and did a double-take. "I hadn't seen you there, buddy," said the cat. "You being the exact same color as the lawn and all... What do you want to know?"

"Where I am, exactly," the turtle repeated. "You see, I seem to have gotten lost."

"Who do you belong to?" asked the cat.

"I don't belong to anyone, sir," said the turtle, slightly offended. "I'm a free turtle."

"A free turtle?" asked the cat with a frown. "You mean... you've walked all the way here from the ocean?"

243

"The ocean?" asked the turtle, licking her lips delightedly. "You mean to tell me there's an ocean nearby?"

"Oh, yeah, sure. But then you probably already knew that, seeing as you come from there."

"Oh, no. I've never seen the ocean in my life, cat."

"Brutus," said the cat.

"Nice to meet you, Brutus. My name is Pinkie."

"So if you weren't born in the ocean, what do you call home?"

"The pond, of course," said Pinkie, wondering if all cats were as slow on the uptake as this one.

"Pond? What pond?"

"Well, *the* pond. Is there any other?"

And seeing as this cat named Brutus hadn't even heard of the pond before, Pinkie figured she might as well return to her slow but sure-footed progress in the direction of wherever it was that her tiny feet were taking her.

"Wait," said Brutus. "Where are you going?"

"You clearly have no idea where the pond is, Brutus," said the tiny turtle, "so I'm guessing you don't know where the ocean is, either."

"Oh, I know where the ocean is, all right."

"You do?"

"Of course."

She mulled this over for a moment. "Would you mind taking me there, Brutus?"

"Um… yeah. Yeah, why not?"

Pinkie smiled. She was a sociable turtle, and appreciated all creatures, great and small. "Thank you, Brutus." She then glanced around and noticed the nice backyard, the nice house, and wondered why a cat would want to leave all that behind to go on a trip with a turtle he barely knew. "Don't you like it here anymore, Brutus?"

"Oh, I like it, I do. But my girlfriend wants to put me on a

EXCERPT FROM PURRFECT FITNESS (THE MYSTERIES OF…

diet of carrots, and between you and me I'm not all that crazy about carrots, so I figured I might as well lay low for a little while, until this latest craze of hers passes—they tend to pass pretty quickly."

"Plenty of food in the ocean," Pinkie said.

"You think?" said Brutus hopefully.

"Oh, sure. Plankton, seaweed, algae, sponges, worms… A regular all-you-can-eat buffet."

Brutus gulped a little. He didn't seem to share Pinkie's excitement for seeking out the ocean, the source of all life, but Pinkie didn't mind. She was sure that Brutus would grow to love the ocean as much as she did. First they had to get there, of course. But she wasn't in any kind of hurry—turtles rarely are. And they'd walked about a foot in ten minutes when Brutus said, "This'll take forever. Why don't I ask one of my humans to take us?"

And so it was that Pinkie was safely seated on the front seat of a nice car, a little old lady behind the wheel, Brutus in the back, the three of them on their way to the ocean.

Life, Pinkie thought as she happily hummed a merry tune, was pretty darn fun.

Chapter Three

"What is a fitness guru, Max?" asked Dooley.

"I think this guy is one, Dooley," I said.

We both sat staring at this new arrival, this star who'd suddenly graced us with his star-studded presence. Odelia and Chase certainly were still in awe, judging from their slack-jawed appearance, and their unusual reluctance to utter a single intelligent word.

"I love your workouts, sir," said Chase, who couldn't stop grinning like a kid now that he'd gotten over his initial shocked surprise at meeting his hero in the flesh. "I've watched all of your YouTube videos and my mom owns all of your videos on VHS—she used to play them to me as a kid, and I just loved watching her work out to them."

"Is that so?" said Mr. Hancock, who'd taken a seat at the living room table, and took this hero-worship in stride with the ease of a man who's been in the limelight for most of his adult life. "They've all been transferred to DVD," he said now. "So you might want to give them to your mom as a birthday present so she can continue her fitness routine."

"Oh, but Mom doesn't work out anymore," said Chase.

"No? And why is that?"

"Her health doesn't allow her to, so…"

"Yeah, I can see how that would complicate things," said the fitness guru politely.

Odelia gestured to the television. "We were just doing one of your routines, sir."

"Just call me Randy, will you?" said the man. "And good for you, Miss Poole."

"Odelia," said Odelia quickly. "And this is Chase. We're your biggest fans, sir—Randy."

"Yes, this is such an honor," Chase gushed.

"That's great," said Randy with a tired smile, then swallowed with a slight sense of unease. He was probably wondering if he'd done the right thing by ringing Odelia's bell. Talking about his workout tapes clearly wasn't what he'd come here for.

"It's so weird to see a person on TV and then to see them in the flesh, Max," said Dooley. "I think he looks better on TV, though."

"That's probably because he was years younger when he taped that video," I said.

"He looks gaunt and pale. And not very fit."

"He just told us he's about to die, Dooley. You wouldn't

look too hot when you only had four more days to live," I pointed out.

A look of concern clouded my friend's face. "Is it cancer, Max? Is Randy Hancock dying from cancer? Or maybe because he did too many of his own workouts and his body simply couldn't take it anymore?"

"I don't know, Dooley," I said. "But the moment Odelia and Chase stop telling him how great they think he is, I'm sure he'll tell us all about it."

Odelia had provided the fitness giant with a glass of freshly squeezed orange juice, and Chase had finally switched off the workout video still playing on the TV, and Randy, who seemed to have calmed down a little, cleared his throat and said, "First off, you have to promise me you won't write a single word I'm going to tell you, Odelia."

"Oh, no, sure," said Odelia, though she looked a little disappointed. The worst thing for a reporter is to have a national celebrity and cultural icon walk into their home and then tell them they can't write all about it in an article.

"If it's medical advice you need, Randy," said Chase, who'd planted one leg firmly on the floor and the other one on a chair, airing his nether regions after the intense workout he'd enjoyed, "just tell us. Odelia's dad is a doctor, you see, and he'll be more than happy to give you a free checkup. Isn't that right, babe?"

"Oh, sure. And I can promise you my dad is very discreet, Randy. Absolutely."

"My health is fine," said Randy with a weak smile. "Though thanks for your concern. No, it's my entourage I'm having trouble with." He heaved a deep sigh. "It's like this. A couple of months ago I accidentally fell from a stepladder and broke my pelvis. The whole thing was extremely painful, and very inconvenient. As you can imagine, a fitness instructor who can't teach his classes anymore, and can't shoot any instructional videos is not much of a fitness instructor. The situation forced me to take it easy for several months while I convalesced at home."

"That must have been terrible, Randy," said Chase with feeling. He looked taken aback that his personal hero proved fallible and had, like all mortals, bones made of, well, bone, and not rubber, as he'd clearly supposed.

"Yeah, well, the incident forced me to take it easy for a while, and it got me thinking. You know, I'm sixty-five years old. I've been in this business for over forty years. Taught thousands and thousands of classes, did more workouts than any other human alive, and so I found myself wondering if maybe, just maybe, it wasn't time for me to take a break."

"A break?" said Chase, looking shocked at this strange conceit. "What do you mean?"

"Retirement, Chase. Hang up my sequin spandex gym shorts and call it quits."

"But… you can't quit, Randy," said Chase. "You're an icon, a monument, a national treasure. As you always say yourself: we should practice fitness until the day we die!"

"Yeah, and of course it's important to stay fit, but the kind of life I was leading wasn't exactly conducive to good health. All this running around, traveling the globe, shooting videos, entertaining people—it's worn me down, Chase. Anyway," he said, waving a hand. "That's not important. What is important is that I told my people that I was quitting. Or at least taking a year or so off to have a think. And that's when all hell broke loose."

"What do you mean?" asked Odelia.

"I'm not sure. All I know is that from the moment I said I was taking a well-deserved break, I started getting threatening letters in the mail, weird phone calls in the middle of the night, and a barrage of emails and private messages on my social media pages."

"Saying what, exactly?" asked Chase.

"Wait, I'll show you," said the fitness man, and took out his phone. "Here—read this."

Chase and Odelia leaned in, and read from Randy's phone. It must have been a doozy, for I saw two jaws drop, and Odelia even clutch a shocked hand to her face in dismay.

"They're all like that," said Randy. "Dozens and dozens of them."

"Randy Hancock we know where you live and you're a dead man," Chase read. "Randy Hancock prepare to die."

"Nice, huh?" He took his phone and scrolled for a moment. "And then last night this came." He placed down the phone and once more Chase and Odelia leaned in curiously.

"Randy Hancock better make your final arrangements for you will die in exactly five days," Odelia read from the man's phone.

"Look at the video," said Randy, patting his fluffy frizzy-haired mane.

Odelia tapped the phone, and a video started playing. All I could hear was the sound, which was awful enough. Like the score of a horror movie, which it probably was.

"Oh, my God," said Odelia.

"No way!" said Chase.

"What's going on!" cried Dooley.

"So you see?" said Randy. "If you don't help me I'll be dead in exactly four days!"

ABOUT NIC

Nic has a background in political science and before being struck by the writing bug worked odd jobs around the world (including but not limited to massage therapist in Mexico, gardener in Italy, restaurant manager in India, and Berlitz teacher in Belgium).

When he's not writing he enjoys curling up with a good (comic) book, watching British crime dramas, French comedies or Nancy Meyers movies, sampling pastry (apple cake!), pasta and chocolate (preferably the dark variety), twisting himself into a pretzel doing morning yoga, going for a run, and spoiling his big red tomcat Tommy.

He lives with his wife (and aforementioned cat) in a small village smack dab in the middle of absolutely nowhere and is probably writing his next 'Mysteries of Max' book right now.

www.nicsaint.com

ALSO BY NIC SAINT

The Mysteries of Max

Purrfect Murder

Purrfectly Deadly

Purrfect Revenge

Purrfect Heat

Purrfect Crime

Purrfect Rivalry

Purrfect Peril

Purrfect Secret

Purrfect Alibi

Purrfect Obsession

Purrfect Betrayal

Purrfectly Clueless

Purrfectly Royal

Purrfect Cut

Purrfect Trap

Purrfectly Hidden

Purrfect Kill

Purrfect Boy Toy

Purrfectly Dogged

Purrfectly Dead

Purrfect Saint

Purrfect Advice

Purrfect Cover

Purrfect Patsy

Purrfect Son

Purrfect Fool

Purrfect Fitness

Box Set 1 (Books 1-3)

Box Set 2 (Books 4-6)

Box Set 3 (Books 7-9)

Box Set 4 (Books 10-12)

Box Set 5 (Books 13-15)

Box Set 6 (Books 16-18)

Box Set 7 (Books 19-21)

Box Set 8 (Books 22-24)

Purrfect Santa

Purrfectly Flealess

Nora Steel

Murder Retreat

The Kellys

Murder Motel

Death in Suburbia

Emily Stone

Murder at the Art Class

Washington & Jefferson

First Shot

Alice Whitehouse

Spooky Times

Spooky Trills

Spooky End

Spooky Spells

Ghosts of London

Between a Ghost and a Spooky Place

Public Ghost Number One

Ghost Save the Queen

Box Set 1 (Books 1-3)

A Tale of Two Harrys

Ghost of Girlband Past

Ghostlier Things

Charleneland

Deadly Ride

Final Ride

Neighborhood Witch Committee

Witchy Start

Witchy Worries

Witchy Wishes

Saffron Diffley

Crime and Retribution

Vice and Verdict

Felonies and Penalties (Saffron Diffley Short 1)

The B-Team

Once Upon a Spy

Tate-à-Tate

Enemy of the Tates

Ghosts vs. Spies

The Ghost Who Came in from the Cold

Witchy Fingers

Witchy Trouble

Witchy Hexations

Witchy Possessions

Witchy Riches

Box Set 1 (Books 1-4)

The Mysteries of Bell & Whitehouse

One Spoonful of Trouble

Two Scoops of Murder

Three Shots of Disaster

Box Set 1 (Books 1-3)

A Twist of Wraith

A Touch of Ghost

A Clash of Spooks

Box Set 2 (Books 4-6)

The Stuffing of Nightmares

A Breath of Dead Air

An Act of Hodd

Box Set 3 (Books 7-9)

A Game of Dons

Standalone Novels

When in Bruges

The Whiskered Spy

ThrillFix

Printed in Great Britain
by Amazon

64031868R00156